Book Cover by G.A. Bellingham

First edition 2026

Atlas Of Imaginary Worlds Publishing

Anatomy

of

Connection

G. A. BELLINGHAM

Atlas of Imaginary Worlds Publishing

'Truth is rarely hidden.

*It is usually placed somewhere people agree
not to look.'*

Chapter One – A Curious Beginning

Mist in Bryngwyn never arrived in the usual fashion. It seeped up from the ground, slow and insistent, as though the village itself exhaled secrets it could no longer contain. On these evenings, the sheep fell silent, and the lanes narrowed into pale corridors, their boundaries uncertain.

Catrin Hughes sat by the fire in her cottage, notebook open but untouched. Coal snapped in the grate, the mantel clock marking each second with mechanical precision. At half-past nine, three measured knocks landed on the oak door.

She recognised the rhythm. Her shoulders relaxed.

"You're late," she said as she drew the bolt.

The visitor entered, shaking droplets from their coat. Firelight caught only the edge of a sleeve, a brief glint from a boot buckle—nothing more.

"You shouldn't have—" Catrin began.

A quiet word interrupted her.

"I see," she replied, her tone sharpening. "But it won't last. Not here. Not in Bryngwyn."

The answer was too low to catch, something about time... or maybe ties.

Catrin shook her head. "No. You can't think it will end well."

Silence settled, broken only by the slow drip of rainwater from the visitor's coat. A chair gave a brief protest as weight shifted. When the figure moved again, it was only to the door.

Catrin let out a small, humourless laugh. "If you're set on it, I won't stop you. But don't expect me to keep quiet."

The latch snapped shut behind them.

When the last ember cracked in the grate, Catrin rose, pulled on her mackintosh, lit the lantern, and stepped into the night. The henhouse waited at the edge of the garden.

Outside, the air carried the taste of wet slate. The henhouse leaned at the garden's edge, tin roof patched with wire, the scent of damp straw rising as she worked. The hens muttered their complaints as she lifted them, her hands brisk, careful.

She set the last egg in her basket. Then—a measured footfall on gravel. Not the uncertain shuffle of a neighbour, nor the quick scatter of a fox. Something heavier. Chosen.

"Who's there?" she called, affecting her usual authority. The tone she used with post-office customers who believed civility was optional.

The mist returned only silence.

The gate creaked. Footsteps crossed the threshold.

"You again," she said, though the words barely found shape. Not out of fear, but more out of calculation. There were debts, favours and negotiations in Bryngwyn that never passed through official channels.

The figure moved forward, stride measured and sure.

Catrin turned before she could see more. The mist tugged at her skirts as she hurried, boots sliding on the slick path. She reached the door, slammed it hard enough to rattle the frame, and shot the bolt across. For a moment, she leaned there, breath sharp, listening to the hush outside.

The first blow shook the frame.

The second cracked the hinge.

The third blow forced the door inward, wood giving with a splintering sigh.

Cold air swept in, mist curling along the floor, the room suddenly unfamiliar.

"Don't be a fool," Catrin snapped, voice sharper now. "This is madness. You'll ruin everything."

The intruder was inside, a presence too large for the small room. The lantern on the table quivered, its flame guttering in the draft. In that brief flicker, a shadow stretched across the wall, an arm lifted, metal glinting once in the light.

The struggle was brief, frantic, and uncoordinated. The lamp toppled, glass scattering across the rug. Furniture scraped stone, a single gasp, then a final, heavy thud.

Then stillness.

Catrin Hughes lay on the parlour floor. Her basket had tipped, eggs scattered, one unbroken, rolling slowly into the edge of the lamplight.

A single folded note slipped from the hearthstone, coming to rest as though placed with care.

Chapter Two — Shadows and Secrets

My phone buzzed at 5:47 AM.

I knew the exact time because I had watched each minute pass since 2:13, when I finally abandoned sleep and began counting the ceiling cracks. There were thirty-seven visible from my bed, branching in a pattern reminiscent of river tributaries on an ordnance survey map. Or perhaps neural pathways in a cross-section, synapses firing in an orderly, predictable rhythm.

The flat was otherwise silent, except for the steady purring of Gwenllian, my rescue tabby, who had installed herself at the foot of my bed during my vigil. Her weight anchored me more effectively than any mindfulness exercise ever had.

"Pryce," I answered, already reaching for my notepad. It lived permanently on the bedside table, its pages filled with observations, phonetic notes, and fragments of unresolved conversations.

DCI Griffith's voice crackled through the speaker, gravelly with too little sleep and too much caffeine.

"Murder in Bryngwyn. Small hamlet west of Lampeter. The victim is a local woman, Catrin Hughes, forty-one. Well, known in the community."

I was already sitting up. "Forensic linguistics required?"

"There's a note. Oddly phrased. Locals aren't sure what to make of it. Tight-knit village. Could be delicate."

The line went dead. That was Griffith's version of encouragement.

I stayed motionless, letting the assignment settle. Rural communities were never as straightforward as they seemed to outsiders. Their language, both spoken and silent, was layered in ways city detectives rarely noticed.

I packed with the same method I always used. Clothes folded along their habitual lines, toiletries sealed against leaks, laptop in its case, digital recorder with new batteries, noise-cancelling headphones. Each item returned to its usual place. The ritual steadied me more than breakfast ever could.

Forty-three minutes later, I boarded the early train into mid-Wales. I took a window seat, not for scenery, but for the defensible angle. The carriage smelled of rain-soaked upholstery and cleaning fluid, with a faint petrol note that was unexpectedly tolerable. The wheels clattered in a steady rhythm, a pattern that did not waver.

The countryside moved past in faded greens and greys. Sheep marked the hills, punctuation in a sentence I had yet to interpret. I noted the change in building materials as we crossed county lines. Old stone surrendered to newer cladding just as a man in a tweed jacket sat opposite me.

"Lovely morning for a trip to the countryside, isn't it?" he said, gesturing toward the window, where the fog pressed against the glass like breath.

I glanced outside. Visibility was poor. Moisture beaded on every surface. "It's extremely low visibility," I replied. "Relative humidity appears close to saturation. I don't understand what that has to do with lovely."

His smile faltered. "Just making conversation, love. Where are you headed? Business or pleasure?"

The endearment tightened something in my jaw. I had never understood why strangers reached for familiarity as if it were a courtesy.

"I can't say either business or pleasure would be accurate descriptions. I'm heading to a murder scene," I replied.

He blinked, then retreated behind his newspaper with the air of someone opting out of a conversation that had ceased to be enjoyable.

Relief settled, quiet and unobtrusive.

The train wound through deep valleys and sudden clearings. I counted seventeen visible churches, their spires faint through the mist. Two hours and seventeen minutes after departure, we eased into Lampeter Station. A young constable in an ill-fitting uniform stood beside a mud-splattered patrol car, holding a laminated sign with my surname written in thick marker.

"You must be DS Pryce," he said, lowering the sign uncertainly. "Sorry. It was the sergeant's idea."

I nodded. "To ensure you don't collect the wrong forensic linguist?"

He blinked, then decided a smile was the safest response.

"We'd better get going. Inspector Vaugh's already at the scene."

Bryngwyn was smaller than I had pictured. People call villages 'quaint,' but this one was simply functional, built from stone that looked older than its inhabitants. The lanes twisted, shaped by repetition rather than design.

The patrol car rolled to a stop outside a cottage that was already attracting spectators. Villagers kept a cautious distance from the police tape, but not enough to hinder observation. In small communities, curiosity is not a vice. It's a form of participation.

DI Gareth Vaugh stepped from the cottage doorway as we approached. Broad-shouldered, raincoat creased at the elbows. His face was set in the practised neutrality that usually covers exhaustion.

"Pryce," he said. "Thanks for coming. This is.... not straightforward."

"Most things aren't," I replied.

He raised an eyebrow, weighing me. People rarely expect that response from female officers, especially those my size. I stopped softening my tone years ago.

"Body is in the parlour," he said. Don't mind the villagers. They've been here since dawn."

"I noticed."

One older man gave us a conspiratorial nod, as if he were on the investigative team.

Inside, the cottage was smaller than it appeared. Low ceilings, stone floor, the last of the fire's warmth still present. The air carried a faint metallic scent, the kind that lingers after violence.

Catrin Hughes lay beside an overturned chair, her coat still on. A broken lamp was scattered across the rug.

Two teacups sat neatly on the table.

"You can see why I asked for your expertise," Vaugh said quietly. "The note's odd."

"Which often means misread," I replied. "People underestimate how rarely language is accidental."

He gestured to the evidence bag on the mantle. I noted its placement without yet asking to examine it.

"My first question," I said, scanning the room, "is simple. Who was she expecting for tea?"

"Exactly," Vaugh said. "She didn't pour that cup for herself."

I crouched near the table, observing the pattern of the liquid rings in the teacups, the symmetry of their placement, and the absence of further disturbance.

"She had a guest," I said. "One she prepared for. And one who stayed long enough to drink."

Vaugh exhaled through his nose. "Welcome to Bryngwyn."

The lamp glass crunched faintly as I stood.

People think rural murders are simple, as if small places are free of complexity.

But they overlook something basic.

In small communities, secrets have shorter distances to travel.

Someone here had closed that distance with care.

Chapter Three — The Village Wakes

By the time I reached the chapel hall, Bryngwyn had already absorbed the event, the way a field takes in rain—quietly, but thoroughly.

PC Ellis opened the chapel door for me. His relief was visible—a task with a clear mechanism, no need for interpretation.

The hall was colder than anticipated. Old stone retained temperature with the persistence of memory—unyielding, even when it served no purpose. My shoes clicked against the floor, the sound lingering a fraction too long. Reverberation was always more pronounced in spaces built for voices.

"We're using the back room," he said. "Inspectors set up in there. Best we could do at short notice." The back room had acquired the look of a temporary headquarters: a table pulled to the centre, plastic chairs arranged with uncertain intent, a whiteboard still faintly marked with last week's hymn numbers, now repurposed for something less routine.

A printed map of Bryngwyn and its outskirts was pinned to one wall. Gareth Vaugh stood at the corkboard, studying the map with the focus of someone practised at letting information wash over him, discarding most of it. I found that quality useful in a colleague.

"You survived the drive," he said.

"PC Ellis appears to view speed limits as flexible suggestions," I replied.

Ellis gave a small cough that might have been contrition or indigestion.

I stepped closer to the map. Clean lines. Edges. Boundaries. Useful structures. Catrin's cottage had been marked with a red pin. So had the vicarage, the post office, the butchers, and the school. A few other points dotted the outskirts – farmhouse, footpaths, the sort of places that existed because weather and geography had collaborated long before planning regulations arrived.

One small blue pin sat alone near the top corner, beside a public footpath. Not labelled. Alone.

"Why blue?" I asked.

Vaugh shrugged. "Just marking points of interest."

"Interest for whom?"

A pause. Half a beat. "Old land boundary. Left over from a survey. Probably nothing."

People often said, "probably nothing" when they meant "something I would prefer not to discuss yet."

I didn't press. Pressing too early blurred the natural pattern formation.

"What's our timeline?" I asked instead.

"Catrin was seen late afternoon in the post office," Vaugh said. Closed up at six. A neighbour heard her in the yard around nine. Doing something with her chickens, apparently. Time of death between nine and ten. The boy found the body at first light. No significant disturbance inside. One broken lamp. The door was forced only after she tried to shut it."

"Guest, not intruder," I said.

"Exactly."

"And the note?" I said.

He gestured to a small evidence table. The bag lay there, neatly labelled.

'Your silence was never worth the price.'

I did not open it yet. Important information needs space to settle before the examination.

"Tea was prepared," Vaugh added. "Two cups. Both were warm when the doctor arrived. Someone drank theirs."

"Catrin didn't," I said.

"No."

I traced the route from the cottage to the lane with my finger. Movement through a village formed its own narrative. Pathways recorded stories that people left unsaid.

'Who noticed the door first?" I asked.

"Boy named Idris. On his way to school early. Says he didn't go inside."

"Believable?"

"Likely. He's eleven. Curiosity at that age is loud, not quiet. He'd have moved something."

I nodded. "We should talk to him later. Children perceive inconsistencies that adults blur."

Vaugh gave me a sidelong look. "You notice a lot of children's behaviour?"

"I notice a lot of patterns," I said.

We both turned to the map again. Bryngwyn was compact. Tightly wound. A cluster of structures knitted close together, as if huddling against weather and memory.

My eye caught a slight marking on the chapel boundary:

Q. Memorial, 1992.

No details. Only a year. Villages tended to catalogue every name, often to excess. Here, the omission was more telling than any inclusion.

But again. It was too early to label significance. The mind's job at this stage was to observe, not decide.

A woman appeared at the doorway holding a tray of steaming mugs. "Tea," she announced, as though presenting evidence.

Vaugh took one. I did not. I preferred consistency in liquid temperature.

"You'll want to start at the post office," he said once the door shut. "Mrs Pritchard knows everything. Or believes she does."

"Belief is often louder than knowledge," I said.

"I suppose you think that's a compliment," Vaugh muttered.

We stepped outside. The drizzle had become a fine mist, collecting on wool and hair, a persistent dampness. In rural Wales, mist was not an atmosphere but a routine, as much a fixture as stone walls or sheep where they were least wanted.

A group of villagers watched from the lane; their expressions arranged into polite disinterest that did not hold. One woman turned her face away the moment I met her eyes. The movement was too quick for embarrassment. Possibly fear. Possibly guilt. Or perhaps nothing at all; people repeated patterns for reasons even they could not name.

"Do you read people this intensely all the time?" Vaugh asked.

"People produce data," I said. "Data wants interpretation."

"Must be tiring."

"Less tiring than being wrong," I said.

His laugh was half a breath. "You really don't ease into things, do you?"

"No," I said truthfully. "I begin where the information begins."

We reached the post office. The door's bell chimed as we stepped inside. The sound was overly cheerful for the atmosphere. Mrs Prichard straightened behind the counter with the eagerness of someone who had been waiting to provide commentary since dawn.

The room smelled of dust, paper, and the faint candy-sweetness of boiled sweets that had been stored for too long. Shelves lined the walls in neat rows. I scanned them unconsciously, assigning each box and packet to its expected purpose.

I did not see Catrin's folder.

But an absence could just be as informative as a presence.

"Detective Inspector," Mrs Prichard said brightly. "And... you must be the expert."

Labels. People used them when they didn't know what else to do.

"DS Pryce," I said. "We'd like to ask you about yesterday."

She folded her hands.

"Oh, love. You'll want to hear everything, I expect."

"I want to hear what's accurate," I said. "Everything comes later."

Her expression shifted. Approval? Amusement? Before she launched into a recollection.

It was immediate, dense and layered more like a verbal avalanche.

I listened carefully.

Separating a signal from noise was familiar work.

Noise could be comforting.

Signals could be dangerous.

And somewhere in her cascade of memory, one detail would eventually matter.

But not quite yet.

This was only the first draft of the truth.

Chapter Four – Mrs Pritchard's Catalogue

"Well then," she said. "You'd best ask what you need. I've been through it all three times this morning and once more while boiling the kettle."

Vaugh's glance was apologetic, almost imperceptibly so. I registered it as a quiet warning, not a reason to pause.

"Let's begin with yesterday afternoon," I said, opening my notebook. "What time did Catrin come in?"

"Four on the dot." Mrs Pritchard nodded emphatically. "She was always precise. Not obsessively so, but enough for you to set your clock by her. Came in with her basket – the one with the willow handle that creaks. And asked for envelopes. The good ones. Thick like. Said she had something 'official' to put in writing."

I made a note of the way she said official, reverence edged with caution, as if such matters had a tendency to linger and return, uninvited.

"Did she say who she was writing to?" I asked.

"No." Another headshake. 'Catrin liked to keep things neat. That included her explanations. She never gave more than necessary. Comes from handling people's business all day, I suppose. Makes you keep your own close."

There was accuracy in her assessment. Proximity to other people's secrets often breeds a kind of guardedness.

"She paid cash?" Vaugh asked.

"Yes, exact change. She always did." Mrs Pritchard's hands fluttered briefly. "And she was…. How shall I put it… sharper than usual. Not unfriendly. Just very *direct*."

Directness, in those unaccustomed to it, often signalled a mind under strain. For someone like Catrin, whose habits were almost structural, it suggested something pressing beneath the surface.

"Did she mention where she was going?" I asked.

"She said she had sorting to finish." Mrs Pritchard pointed to the shelves behind her with something that was not quite exasperation. "She'd taken it upon herself to reorganise the old storage boxes. Not the modern ones. The ones that nobody's touched since the nineties. Kept muttering about mismatched dates and incomplete lists."

"What sort of lists? I asked.

"Oh, you know. Parcel logs, compensation forms, and delivery receipts. Some of them are so old that the ink is nearly gone. I told her half of it was irrelevant, but Catrin had a way of deciding something wasn't irrelevant anymore."

Irrelevance is a matter of perspective. Catrin's definition, I suspected, diverged from the village consensus.

"Was anyone else here when she came in?" Vaugh asked.

"No," Mrs Pritchard said. "Quiet afternoon. Everyone was at choir practice or tending livestock or pretending not avoid each other, as usual."

I studied the back shelves. Order prevailed, but not everywhere. Some rows carried Catrin's signature precision; others leaned, just enough to betray years of inattention.

On the lowest shelf, a rectangular absence remained, the dust still undisturbed at its edges.

"What was kept there?" I asked, pointing.

Mrs Pritchard followed my gesture, then frowned. "That was one of the older folders. The blue-backed one. Thick. Fell to bits last year. I taped the spine. Catrin used it a few times for reference."

"What kind of reference?" I asked.

"Old paperwork from before I took over." She waved a hand dismissively. "Bits of things. Old parish correspondence. A few clippings about village events. Nothing dramatic. The sort of history nobody bothers with."

"Is it missing? Vaugh asked gently.

Mrs Pritchard's pause lasted half a breath too long.

"I assume so," she said finally. "Unless one of you took it."

"We haven't removed anything," Vaugh said.

"Then someone's been in here," Mrs Pritchard said matter-of-factly. "I locked up at half five. Opened at eight. That space wasn't empty yesterday."

I watched her face. No trace of worry, only a practical acceptance.

"Is the key to the front door ever left on the premises?" I asked.

"Not once," she said. "Not even during the Jubilee when everyone else was tipsy. I keep it in my handbag at home."

"Who had entry then?" I asked.

"Well." She exhaled. "That's the odd bit. The Reverend stopped by this morning. Before I'd even turned the kettle on."

A flicker of attention passed through Vaugh's stance. Not suspicion, exactly—more the mental act of filing something for later.

"Did he go behind the counter?" Vaugh asked.

"He leaned," she said. "And I turned away to get him a stamp. I don't suspect him. But he was close enough."

Proximity was not proof, but it was rarely irrelevant.

"What did he want? I asked.

"To post a letter, she said. "Rather short one. Very crisp handwriting. He looked like he'd had a rough night. More thinking than sleeping if you know what I mean."

It was a telling observation—disarray of feeling, not of appearance.

"Did he see Catrin's sorting?" I asked.

"Oh, he saw all sorts of things." Mrs Pritchard lowered her voice. "She asked him about some older documents last week. Parish notices. He'd gone a bit pale, but he said it was 'all very unimportant.' Which is the exact phrasing people use when something is extremely important?"

She had a knack for stumbling onto the heart of things, even unintentionally.

"Did Catrin seem worried recently?" I asked.

"No," Mrs Pritchard said. "More.. determine as if she'd found something she didn't quite understand yet but wanted to. She was making sense of something, but she wasn't ready to say what."

"That fits her temperament?" I asked.

"Oh yes," Mrs Pritchard said. "Catrin didn't like loose ends. She said a thing half-known is worse than a thing fully known."

"And yesterday evening?" Vaugh said. "Did she lock up normally?"

"She always did," Mrs Pritchard said. 'Double-check, turn the sign, latch the door. She was a creature of habit."

"Who benefits from her habits?" I asked.

"Everyone," Mrs Pritchard said. "Which is why it is so upsetting." She pressed her palms together. "You know what people are like in small places. They rely on the ones who keep things quiet."

"Quiet?" I repeated.

"Quietly running," she clarified. "Same thing here."

I marked the distinction.

Quiet.

Quietly running.

Quietly kept.

Quietly corrected.

Silence, in a village, was never singular.

Catrin had unsettled one variety.

'And you are certain nothing else is missing?" Vaugh asked.

"Certain?" She scoffed. "I'm certain of very little these days. Except that Catrin had been looking at things older than she was, and now those things are suddenly relevant to someone else."

She folded her arms.

"Do you think whatever she was sorting is why she's dead? She asked us.

"We're exploring all possibilities," Vaugh said.

I left the question alone. The phrase 'exploring all possibilities' covered both too much and not enough.

We stepped outside, having thanked her. The drizzle had refined itself, so fine it registered as texture rather than weather.

Vaugh exhaled, the sound neither relief nor frustration—just a release.

"Well," he said. "That was…"

"Informative," I supplied.

"Exhausting," he corrected.

"Both can be true."

He huffed a short laugh. "Did you get all that?"

"Most," I said. "Some details I'm reserving for later examination."

"And the folder?"

"Yes," I said. "And its absence."

We walked a few steps in silence.

"What do you think?" he asked.

"I think," I said carefully, "that Catrin Hughes was trying very hard to understand something she believed mattered – and someone else believed did not."

"Or believed that it should not," Vaugh added.

"That possibility as well."

He nodded, rubbing his jaw.

"School next?" he asked.

"Yes," I said. "Order of relevance."

As we turned onto the lane, I saw the chapel plaque again.

1992.

Still with no names.

A detail, patient, awaiting its moment.

I didn't look at it for long.

Patterns were beginning to coalesce.

But patterns were not conclusions.

Not yet.

Chapter Five – Margins of Error

The school perched at the crest of Bryngwyn's main lane, stone walls scrubbed but pitted by rain. Inside, the paint would be fresh; outside, the years had done their quiet work. Four murals faced the road: dragons, daffodils, and children in a ring. Their colours had been rinsed to pastel by persistent drizzle.

Vaugh held the gate open for me. It squeaked with a tone that was neither pleasant nor alarming, simply persistent. A sound that had learned patience from Welsh rain.

"Rhian Lewis should be in early," he said. "She's the sort who prefers classrooms to be tidy before the children arrive."

"Anticipatory order," I said. "Useful for environments with unpredictable variables."

"Children," he translated.

"Yes."

We took the narrow path to the door. Damp leaves pressed their scent into the air, undercut by a faint thread of diesel from somewhere beyond the fields. Inside, the hallway absorbed sound unevenly, as rural schools do—too much in some corners, not enough in others.

Children's drawings lined the walls—dragons, castles, rainbows with colours out of order. Some were careful. Others ignored the edges entirely. I found Samuels's work at once: clean lines, repeating shapes, a kind of internal logic. Rhian had said he drew often. His drawings stood out, not by design, but by nature.

Rhian was alone in her classroom, sorting worksheets into quiet stacks. The air held disinfectant, pencil shavings, and a trace of sweetness—fruit peel, maybe, left to soften in the bin overnight.

She looked up as we entered.

"Oh," she said softly, tucking a loose strand of hair behind her ear. "Inspector Vaugh. And you must be DS Pryce."

She said my name with no hesitation, no visible attempt to memorise it first. Not all adults did that.

"Yes," I said. "Thank you for meeting us."

Rhian stepped away from her desk, folding her hands loosely in front of her. She had the quiet, composed posture of someone who spent considerable energy maintaining consistency for other people's benefit.

"What can I help with?" she asked.

"Catrin Hughes," Vaugh said. "We understand you saw her yesterday."

"Yes." A soft nod. "She dropped off some community notices for the board outside. Wanted them posted before next week. Something about a council meeting."

Her eyes flicked toward the window, where the notice board sat half-obscured by fog. "She said she wanted things to be 'in order'. That was her phrasing."

In order. Not unusual for Catrin, by all accounts. But the phrase kept surfacing, echoing between witnesses. It meant something.

"And how did she seem?" I asked.

"Preoccupied," Rhian said. "Not worried. Just...aligning something in her head."

I noted her word: aligning. Not a feeling, but a process. Most people described emotions. Rhian described cognition. Noted.

"Did she say what she was aligning?" I asked.

"No," she said. "She rarely elaborated unless you pressed, and pressing usually made her retreat."

I understood. Explaining things could feel like surrendering the shape of your own thoughts.

"Did she talk to anyone else here?" Vaugh asked.

"Briefly to the caretaker," Rhian said. "But only about the usual. Deliveries: The boiler is making that clicking noise again. Nothing unusual."

She hesitated. The pause outlined what she left unsaid.

"But she did ask me... something odd," Rhian added.

"What was that?" I asked.

"She asked if the school still kept old attendance logs. The handwritten ones from before we digitised everything."

"And do you?" I asked.

"No," Rhian said. "All the older logs were sent to storage years ago. Council warehouses. No one's bothered since."

"Did Catrin explain why she wanted them?" Vaugh asked.

"No." Her hands tightened slightly on the edge of a desk. "She only said she was 'checking a few dates."

Dates. Another pattern. She was matching, reconciling—something unfinished.

"And was this unusual for her?" I asked.

Rhian thought for a moment. "Not entirely. Catrin was…" She paused, searching for a description. "A person who liked things to match. Calendar dates, ledger entries, names in the right places. She didn't tolerate gaps."

"Did that ever cause friction?" Vaugh asked.

"Not friction," Rhian said carefully. "But… discomfort. Some people prefer their pasts left a little blurry."

The words left a faint resonance in the room.

"Your father knew her?" Vaugh said.

Rhian blinked at the shift. "Everyone knew her."

"That's not what I asked," Vaugh said gently.

She drew in a breath. "He did, yes. They served on several committees together years ago. Fundraisers, garden projects, things like that."

"Did Catrin ever ask you about him?" I asked.

"No," she said firmly. Then her gaze flicked downward for a microsecond. But just enough to signal an internal correction.

"She asked me once," Rhian amended. "But it was nothing unusual. She was tracing old committee minutes to update the chapel's noticeboard history."

"Did she even mention what she found?" I asked.

"No." A small swallow. "But she had that look. The one she got when she'd spotted something out of place."

"Out of place how?" I asked.

"Out of place in a way she didn't want to voice yet," Rhian said, "There's a difference."

I marked the detail.

Rhian registered tension others left unspoken.

She was observant.

Perhaps too observant for someone who claimed not to understand Catrin's preoccupation.

"May we see Samuel?" I asked.

"After break," Rhian said. "He's in his quiet routine right now. He will talk more freely if we let him finish it."

A correct inference.

Interrupting routine sends ripples through cognition.

She retrieved a sheet of paper from her desk, a drawing.

"This is what he brought in this morning," she said softly. "I didn't ask him about it. I thought you might prefer to see it unfiltered."

The drawing was simple. Striking.

A door.

A figure outside.

Another figure inside.

Lines radiating outward. Not decorative lines, but motion lines. Lines radiated outward. Not decoration—motion. Impact. Force. Answer.

I was studying the angle.

Samuel had captured physics, unintentional but exact.

He'd stretched the doorway, the top tilting inward—child's perspective from below.

Perspective: child-height.

"This is helpful," I said.

"I hoped so," Rhian said. "Samuel doesn't lie. Not even to be polite."

A truth, quietly certain.

"Did Catrin ever mention Samuel specifically?" I asked.

"She always brought him little things," Rhian said. "Post office stickers, old postcards, once a packet of foreign stamps someone never collected. She understood him."

"Understood him how?" I asked.

"She understood that he didn't need to be coaxed into being someone else, " Rhian said.

"She simply accepted who he was."

A flicker in her tone. Respect, or grief. Possibly both.

"She did that for a lot of people," Rhian added more quietly. "Even when they didn't deserve it."

The room contracted, her words displacing air.

"Thank you," I said. "We'll speak with Samuel next."

"Of course," Rhian said. "Please… be gentle with him. He sees things very sharply. Sharper than most."

I nodded.

"I've noticed."

She offered a ghost of a smile. Sad, restrained, genuine.

As Vaugh and I stepped out of the classroom, the hallway stretched ahead like a spine with branching ribs. Children's voices filtered faintly through the building as classes prepared for break. "You think she's hiding something?" Vaugh asked under his breath as we walked.

"Everyone is hiding something," I said.

"Yes, yes, you've told me that before."

"But some people," I added, "are hiding different *kinds* of things."

"And Rhian?"

"She's not hiding guilt," I said. "She's hiding the shape of something she hasn't fully confronted."

"That's even more cryptic."

"Precision often is," I said.

We stepped into a light breeze. Moisture sharpened the grass, made it gleam. A sheep complained nearby, persistent as if that were its only purpose.

Walking toward the playground, I glanced back. Rhian watched from the window, one hand braced on the sill, steadying herself.

"She knows more than she realises," I said.

"Or less," Vaugh countered.

"Both possibilities are compatible."

He groaned. "I'm not sure if you're brilliant. Or unbearable."

"Both possibilities are compatible," I repeated.

The unexpected sound of Vaugh's laugh cut through the morning air.

We continued toward the small sensory room, where Samuel waited. Quiet, observant, precise.

A witness who would give us the next piece.

Chapter Six – Samuel's Lines and Silences

The sensory room hid behind the main corridor. Small, constructed with more understanding than the rest of the school managed. Soft lighting. Muted colours. Low shelves, arranged with deliberate intent. A beanbag slumped in one corner, deflating but still maintaining its outline. The air carried a trace of fabric cleaner. Possibly, beneath that, the waxy scent of crayons, residual warmth from small hands.

Samuel Lang sat cross-legged on the carpet, absorbed in the act of colouring. His crayons formed a gradient: warm to cool, light to dark. Not order for its own sake. A system. The distinction was important.

He did not look up when Vaugh and I entered. Expected. Task focus overrode environmental change.

I crouched, choosing a position at the edge of intrusion—close enough for conversation, distant enough for comfort. My knees protested.

Vaugh hovered by the door, his presence tilting the room's balance.

Samuel shaded the upper corner of a doorway in his drawing. Perspective: child's eye level. Slight inward tilt. Accurate to lived experience.

"Hello, Samuel," I said quietly.

He didn't answer.

But he shifted to a darker crayon.

Shoreline of attention acknowledged.

"You can keep drawing," I said. "Talking isn't required."

A half-second pause, then he chose another crayon. Consent.

Silence. Not the brittle adult variety. Productive.

Then:

"When a door breaks," Samuel said without lifting his gaze, "it makes two noises."

Vaugh stiffened behind me.

"Two?" I asked.

"Yes."

He drew a firm horizontal line.

"Wood first. Then metal."

"The latch," I said.

He nodded. "And the bottom hinge. It sticks when it's cold."

Cold hinge. Season. Temperature. All catalogued in his memory.

"Where were you?" I asked.

"In the lane."

He frowned slightly. "Mum says don't dawdle in fog. But I had to draw the moon first."

"Draw the moon?"

"On my hand."

He held it up: a faint crescent indentation on his palm.

"Nights until Friday."

Systematic.

I respected the system.

"What time was it?" Vaugh asked.

"Dark-o'clock," Samuel said.

Then, after consideration, "Before chickens stop talking. Not night-night. The other one."

"Dusk," I said.

He relaxed. Definitions provided footholds.

"What did you hear before the two noises?" I asked.

He paused, eyes unfocused, as people do when rewinding auditory memories.

"Talking voice. Only one."

"Catrin?" Vaugh asked.

"Yes. Telling hens to be quiet."

"And the other person?" I prompted.

"Not mouth-talking."

He tapped his fingertips on the floor.

"Feet-talking. Crunch-crunch. Slow crunch."

The mimicry was perfect.

"Could you see them?" I asked.

"Fog ate the edges," he said. "It does that."

"Yes," I said. "Fog blurs shapes first."

He nodded approvingly.

"But you *did* see something?" I asked.

"A coat," he said. "Long. Straight. Like a rectangle with arms."

"Colour?" Vaugh asked.

"Dark. Like the bins on Wednesday."

Sufficiently specific.

"And anything else?" I asked.

Samuel used a new crayon. A soft graphite grey. To draw a circle on the shoulder of the coat.

"That," he said.

"A circle?" I asked.

"Yes."

"Badge?" Vaugh guessed.

Samuel shook his head. "Not a badge. Sewn-on. Not shiny. Not a sticker. Sew-seen."

"What shape inside the circle?" I asked.

He shrugged slightly. "Leaf shape. But not leaf. Like the old sign."

"What sign?" Vaugh asked.

He flicked a hand toward the window. "The footpath one. The scratchy sign with the chipped paint."

I stored the details without responding externally.

"What did you see after the noises?" I asked.

He drew a line across the doorway. Clean. Heavy.

"Nothing," he said. "Like the world stopped talking."

Stillness. The room recalibrated.

"And then?" I asked.

"Fog moves when someone walks through it," he said, as if explaining something basic. "It folds. You can see it if you squint."

He squinted.

Demonstration.

"And you saw fog fold?' I asked.

"Yes. Twice."

Two movements.

In.

Out.

"And then?" Vaugh asked softly.

"Then the chickens shouted."

He coloured a burst of lines around the bottom corner of the door.

Motion, rendered.

Or panic, visualised.

"Samuel," I said after a moment. "May we take your pictures with us to look at?"

He held the page out stiffly, not quite toward me, not quite toward Vaugh.

"Don't bend it," he instructed.

"We won't," Vaugh said, treating the drawing as though it were a legal artefact.

Samuel turned back to his crayons.

He selected a new colour. Deep teal. Began to draw the fog.

Layered.

Soft.

Precise.

A visual transcript of auditory recall.

We stepped into the hallway, and the door closed behind us with a soft click.

Vaugh exhaled. Relief at leaving a charged environment.

"He's extraordinary," Vaugh said.

"He's accurate," I corrected. "Accuracy is often mistaken for extraordinariness."

"And the patch? The coat?"

"Possibilities," I said. "Not conclusions."

"And the footpath sign?" he nudged.

But I didn't answer that one.

Premature anchoring of possibilities: a risk.

We walked down the hallway lined with artwork.

Some of the paintings were chaotic.

Some literal.

One drawing. A house with an excess of windows. Registered, briefly.

Children often added windows when they felt things were being watched.

Noted.

Not interpreted.

Outside, the wind intensified. Metallic trace from distant farm machinery.

The sky: tin-coloured. Unchanged.

"Next stop: the Reverend," Vaugh said.

"Yes."

"You're not looking forward to that," he observed.

"I don't look forward or backward," I said. "Only laterally."

He blinked. "What does that mean?"

'It means his reactions may complicate the data."

"And this folder you think he took?" Vaugh asked.

"No," I said. "I don't think he took the folder."

"Then what?"

"He took context," I said. "Context is more dangerous to investigations than missing objects."

He frowned. "I don't follow."

"You will."

We reached the bend in the lane.

There, half-hidden in ferns, stood the old footpath sign.

Its paint is barely visible.

Circular emblem.

Leaf-shaped interior.

Weathered nearly to nothing.

Most walked past without seeing anything.

Samuel, however, had seen structure.

Children often did.

The sign leaned slightly.

Tilted.

As if recording years of wind and neglect.

Vaugh didn't notice it at all.

Good.

"Ready?" he asked as we approached the vicarage gate.

"Yes," I said.

Internally, I sorted Samuel's observations into their respective compartments.

A door.

Two noises.

Fog folding.

A long coat.

A circular patch.

And a child's quiet certainty.

Not a conclusion.

Not yet.

But an angle.

An orientation of the truth.

Bryngwyn, fog and silence notwithstanding, was beginning to reveal its underlying pattern.

Chapter Seven – The Reverend's Revision

The vicarage sat slightly apart from the rest of Bryngwyn, as though the house itself had stepped back a pace to observe the village with polite caution. It was a modest stone building softened by climbing ivy and years of Welsh weather. The garden showed signs of recent attention. The beds are newly turned, the lingering scent of compost. But the tools resting by the shed were arranged with a precision that suggested someone had stopped halfway through a task.

The Reverend answered the door, already unsettled.

Not startled. Displaced. The look of someone pulled from a thought that had resisted resolution.

His smile was polite but held too tightly at the corners.

"Inspector Vaugh," he said. "And…yes, you must be DS Pryce. Come in. Terrible business. I hardly slept."

He said it with the cadence of someone who expected sympathy but wasn't sure how to ask for it.

"We won't take much of your time," Vaugh said.

That was a lie. We would take as long as needed.

Predictability rarely served interviews.

The sitting room pressed in with heat. The fire burned, unnecessary for the mild morning. Coal smoke and lavender polish mingled in the air. A teapot waited on a tray, two cups—one used, one untouched. A book, open and face down on the side table. *Lives of the Saints*. The bookmark is halfway through.

He was reading about martyrs.

Not necessarily relevant.

Possibly relevant.

"Please, sit."

He gestured to the armchairs. Vaugh took one. I sat on the edge of the sofa, feet flat, careful. The carpet's thick pile held small, irregular dents—interruptions in an otherwise disciplined surface.

"Reverend Thomas," Vaugh said, "We understand you saw Mrs Pritchard this morning?"

"Yes," the Reverend answered quickly. "I posted a letter—routine diocesan admin. I wanted to send it promptly."

"Before opening hours?" Vaugh asked casually.

"I was passing." He smiled tightly. "I'm often awake early."

His hands were smooth. No soil beneath the nails. No new calluses. The tools outside told a different story.

Meticulous washing, or the gardening was for show.

"You mentioned you're often awake early," I said. "Did you see or hear anything unusual last night?"

He hesitated. A slight, fractional pause. "I...no. Nothing. I was indoors all evening. Preparing my sermon. A quiet night."

Too quick. Too neat.

Information, but no texture.

"Did you speak to Catrin recently?" I asked.

"Yes," he said softly, folding his hands together. "Last week. She asked me about old parish notices. Wanted to confirm dates for some historical display she was planning."

"What kind of display?" Vaugh asked.

"Oh, just the usual village heritage exhibition." His voice thinned slightly.

"She liked things presented accurately. Down to the month. Sometimes the day."

"And did that trouble you?" I asked.

"Trouble?" He blinked. "No. Just unnecessary. Old matters are often better left where they rest."

A harmless statement. Except when it wasn't.

"What did she want clarification on?" I asked.

"Oh… only trivial things. Fetes. Committee minutes. Nothing of consequence."

A contradiction. Earlier, he had said less was better. Now, he claimed irrelevance.

"What about old inspection reports?" I asked lightly.

His throat tightened. Barely visible, but there.

"I'm not familiar with those," he said too quickly. "Inspection reports are council matters, not parish."

My notebook stayed closed on my lap. Writing too soon disrupted the act of seeing.

"You seemed...uncomfortable when she brought those up," I said.

He swallowed. "Not uncomfortable. Merely surprised. She had a way of asking questions that made you feel inspected yourself."

Rhian had described something similar. Not fear. Discomfort.

"But you helped her?" Vaugh asked.

"Of course." He forced a smile. "I help everyone."

His eyes did not match his smile.

"Did she mention anything else?" I asked.

"No. Nothing significant."

He paused. "She was organising a collection of documents, I think. She didn't elaborate. Not the folder.

But perhaps the subject.

May I ask?" he said suddenly, turning to me, "Why are you here? I mean, not your role, but your presence. Specifically."

I met his gaze evenly.

"My expertise is linguistic and behavioural analysis."

"Ah." A flicker of unease. "So, you examine… how people choose their words."

"Yes," I said. "And how they choose their silences."

A sheen of perspiration appeared at his temple.

Just enough to register.

Not enough to justify environmental heat.

"I see," he said quietly.

I suspect he did.

"There's been talk," he went on. "That Catrin was…. stirring things. Asking questions that are best left alone. I don't know who starts these rumours, but I assure you, I discouraged nothing."

He had used the phrase 'best left alone'. Twice now.

A pattern.

"What concerns you about her questions?' I asked.

His mouth tightened.

"I don't like unnecessary disturbance. This village has… a delicate history."

Vaugh shifted. "What part of its history?"

The Reverend picked up the cooling teacup, set it down again. A displacement behaviour.

"Oh. Simply old matters. Old events. Misunderstandings that were resolved decades ago."

Another evasion.

Another shaped silence.

"Would those be parish matters?" I asked.

"All matters are parish matters in a village," he replied automatically, before seeming to regret the honesty.

I watched him. Micro-tensions in his posture.

He was not lying to protect himself.

He lied to protect a *narrative*.

"Reverend," I said softly. "Did Catrin ask you about anything that made you uncomfortable?"

His eyes dropped to his clasped hands.

"Not uncomfortable," he said. "Just.... Unsettled."

He hesitated. Too long.

Then:

"She asked about the memorial plaque."

There it was.

But softly.

Almost accidental.

"The one on the chapel wall," he clarified.

"From 1992?" I asked.

"Yes." His voice shrank. "It… commemorates an event the village doesn't revisit often."

"What event?" Vaugh asked.

The Reverend straightened abruptly.

"It's not relevant to the case."

"You don't get to decide that," Vaugh said mildly.

The Reverend's composure fluttered.

Only for a heartbeat.

But I saw it.

He looked at me then, not Vaugh.

"Some tragedies," he said with quiet firmness.

"Don't need to be re-examined."

"Some do," I said, "Especially when someone else begins to."

His jaw tightened.

He knew exactly what I meant.

He was not the murderer.

But he was the archivist of a truth he did not want unlocked.

"We'll need to speak again," Vaugh said, rising.

"Of course," the Reverend murmured. "I'm at your disposal."

He wasn't.

He would resist.

But politely.

Outside, the cold air was clean. Sharper after the vicarage's suffocating warmth.

Vaugh exhaled. "Well. He's hiding something."

"Yes," I said. "But not violence."

"You're sure?"

"He hides the past," I said. "Not the present."

Vaugh digested that in silence as we walked down the lane.

Bryngwyn felt smaller now.

Constricted.

The cottages seemed to huddle closer, as if they sensed something shifting beneath their foundations.

Samuel's drawing rustled in Vaugh's hand.

"Now what?" he asked.

"We follow the timeline," I said. "And look for the person whose fear of the truth takes a different shape."

"Differently how?"

"The Reverend fears disruption," I said.

"Another person fears exposure."

"Exposure of what?"

"Something in those old reports. A mistake," I said. "One that someone believes would not survive daylight."

We continued toward the crossroads, and fog drifted in slow currents around us.

Not a conclusion.

But the edges of one.

The village, like a sentence written too tightly, had started to show where the grammar failed to hold.

Chapter Eight- The Butcher Who Knew Better

The butcher's shop marked the crossroads, a full stop in Bryngwyn's map. Square, solid, its windows blurred by the clash of cold glass and wet morning air. Above the door, HUGHES AND SONS, the red paint faded and the H chipped, so the name hovered between statement and uncertainty.

Dylan Hughes wiped the counter as we entered. He stood tall, shoulders shaped by years of lifting unwilling weight and bending over a counter built for someone smaller. Grey threaded his hair at the temples. His apron bore the ghost of old stains, scrubbed but never erased. His hands were carved, large and capable, the kind that could break or mend with equal ease.

He looked up as the bell on the door chimed.

"Inspector," he said with a short nod. "And... the other one."

"DS Pryce," Vaugh supplied. "We need a moment."

Dylan returned to wiping the counter, his movements deceptively slow.

Not deflective. More controlled.

"I heard," he said. "About Catrin. Terrible. She didn't deserve that."

"How well did you know her?" Vaugh asked.

"Well enough," Dylan said. "Everyone knows everyone here. Except when they pretend otherwise."

A burr of irritation edged his words. Not for us. For the village itself, as if Bryngwyn were a person who let him down repeatedly.

"And recently?" I asked.

He scrubbed a faint mark on the metal surface, though it didn't require scrubbing. "She came in last week for stew beef. Told me I should label things better on the front counter because the prices don't match the sheet in the window."

"Did that bother you?" Vaugh asked.

"No," Dylan said. "Because she was right. But people don't like being righted. Especially not here."

His jaw set. Dylan was not the type to bristle at correction. He noticed when others did.

"Did you see her yesterday?" I asked.

"Not in the shop," he said. "But I saw her walking down the lane late afternoon. Looked focused. Basket on her arm. Head down. She walked like someone who'd just made a decision."

I noted that.

People called Catrin preoccupied. Resolved. Aligning something unseen.

Those were cognitive descriptors.

Unusual, here. Gossip prefers adjectives that bruise, not ones that map the mind.

"Did she speak to anyone while you watched her?" I asked.

"No," Dylan said. "She walked straight past Eifion at the corner. Didn't even look at him."

"Eifion Davies?" Vaugh asked. "The man with the limp?"

"Yes," Dylan said. "He was heading this way. She didn't stop for him. Not like her. She usually had a word for everyone."

"Any reason she might have avoided him?" I asked.

Dylan hesitated.

"She'd asked him something last week," he said finally. "Something about old compensation records."

I didn't speak.

I didn't need to.

I let Dylan fill the silence.

He exhaled.

"She asked about dates, delivery dates, and inspection dates. Eifion said she was poking her nose somewhere it didn't belong."

"And was she?" Vaugh asked.

"That depends on who you ask," Dylan said.

His voice darkened slightly.

He wasn't angry at Catrin.

He was angry at what she'd stepped into.

"Did Eifion seem upset?" I asked.

"He always seemed upset," Dylan said. "But yes. More than usual. He used to work up near the quarry. The old one."

"And yesterday?" Vaugh asked. "Where was Eifion in the evening?"

"No idea," Dylan said. "Ask his wife. She'll give you an answer whether it's true or not."

The corner of my mouth shifted.

Not a smile. Not yet.

"Did *you* see anything last night?" I asked.

He leaned against the counter, the rag hanging loosely from his hand.

"No," he said. "But the dogs barked around nine. The whole row heard them."

"Dogs?" Vaugh echoed.

"Davies' dogs. The bark at anything," Dylan said.

A pause.

"But this was different. Short bark, then silence. They only do that when someone familiar walks by."

I let that settle.

Dogs sense belonging before people do.

"And what about you?" I asked.

"Did you hear anything else?"

His brows drew together.

"I heard something like… a crack. Not loud. More like wood shifting."

"Like a door?" Vaugh asked.

"Maybe," Dylan said. "But sound carries strangely in fog. Makes things fold in on themselves."

Samuel's phrase echoed: *Fog eats the edges*.

"And did you see anyone near Catrin's?" I asked.

"No," he said. "But there was someone in a long coat heading up the lane earlier in the evening. Dark coat. Couldn't see their face."

"A man?" Vaugh asked.

"Didn't walk like a man," Dylan said simply.

I met his eyes.

"Explain," I said.

He shrugged one muscular shoulder. "Gait was too light. Shoulders narrower. Footfall pattern shorter. Could've been a teenager. Could've been a woman. Wasn't a heavy stride."

Not a man.

Not conclusive.

But directional.

"Anything else?" I asked.

"Yes," he said after a moment's internal debate.

"She had a folder with her last week."

"What folder?" Vaugh asked.

"A blue one," Dylan said. "Old. Held together with tape. Stuffed full of old papers."

A small knot formed in my chest.

"And?" I asked.

"She said she needed 'just one more thing' before she posted it somewhere."

"Somewhere?" Vaugh repeated.

"She didn't say. Just... somewhere."

Not to the Reverend.

Not to Mrs Pritchard.

Not to the council.

Somewhere else.

"And this was last week?" I asked.

"Yes."

"Did she still have the folder yesterday?" I asked.

"I didn't see her carrying it."

That was worse, somehow.

It meant the folder was in her cottage, waiting to be found,

or already gone before she died.

"Dylan," Vaugh said, "did she seem frightened lately?"

"No," he said.

But his eyes shifted. Just slightly.

"Not frightened. Just... done with waiting. You know the look people get when they've realised something they can't un-realise?"

He noticed what others missed.

"And you?" I asked. "What have you realised?"

He gave a short, humourless laugh. "That Bryngwyn hasn't told the truth about anything important in years."

We let silence do the work.

The butcher understood the village's decay better than the Reverend ever would.

"Last question," Vaugh said, "Is there anything you're not telling us?"

"Loads," Dylan said. "But none of it's relevant to killing Catrin."

"Why not?" I asked.

He wiped his hands on his apron again.

"Because the person who killed her didn't do it for money or anger."

"Then what?" Vaugh asked.

"For fear," Dylan said quietly. "Something she touched scared someone who doesn't scare easily."

That was a precise deduction.

Almost disquieting.

"And you know this how?" I asked.

He met my gaze squarely.

"Because Catrin wasn't the kind of woman who tripped over danger," he said.

"She walked straight into it."

We left. The doorbell's brittle jingle trailed behind, too light for what we carried out.

Outside, the fog loosened its grip. Not gone, just drawn back, like a quilt from a restless sleeper. The lane waited, damp and unchanged, or pretending to be.

Vaugh blew out a breath. "So now we've got Eifon, the Reverend, Rhian, and half the village acting strange."

"No," I said. "We have patterns."

"Which ones?"

"Discomfort. Raised defences. Narrative inconsistencies. Emotional displacement."

"And the murdered?" he asked.

"Not yet," I said. "But we're circling the right orbit."

We walked on.

Past the chapel.

Past the footpath sign.

Past the memorial, where no one was named.

Truth lived somewhere in Bryngwyn's bones.

Not visible yet.

But present.

A shape waited beneath the fog.

Chapter Nine – The Note That Didn't Fit

Catrin Hughes's cottage sat on a slight rise above the lane, its garden gate leaning outward as if trying to escape the house's grief. The path leading to the front door was scattered with grit where officers had walked earlier, the uniform pattern now interrupted by random footprints. The forensics van had gone. The tape was still up.

The house was quiet in the way that follows intrusion. Air held, as if the rooms waited for someone to explain the new disorder.

Vaugh unlocked the door. The hinges complained softly.

Inside, the air was stale. Not with the weight of neglect, but with the abruptness of interruption. A life left unfinished.

Lavender polish lingered beneath the sharper note of poultry feed. A coat and scarf hung in careful alignment. The hallway did not belong to a woman who died in chaos. Her order persisted wherever the murderer had not reached.

The living room was another matter.

A lamp, broken at the base, spilled white porcelain across the hearth. A chair stood at an unnatural angle. The rug was just off its axis. Subtle, but visible to anyone who noticed patterns.

Serene Pryce always knew where to look.

I stepped around the fragments, not to preserve evidence—the forensics team had already left— but because breaking patterns unsettled me.

A small ceramic hen sat on the mantel; its wing mended with a thin line of glue. The break was old. Catrin had chosen to repair, not replace.

"Look familiar?" Vaugh asked.

"It looks like Catrin's handwriting," I said. "But something is off."

The note lay inside an evidence sleeve on the coffee table, its single fold crisp.

Vaugh placed it gently in front of me.

Small, neat handwriting, slanting just to the right. Blue ballpoint ink. The message:

'Truth makes cowards of the unprepared.'

Not Shakespeare. People often thought so, but the original line was different. This was constructed to sound literary, but it was only an imitation.

"Her phrasing?" Vaugh asked.

No. Catrin's notes chose clarity over flourish. Grocery lists, community notices—always functional. This was written to perform.

"And she didn't seem the theatrical sort to you?" Vaugh asked.

"No," I said. "But someone wanted to sound like they were.

"What does that tell you?"

The author wanted to seem educated, but the effect was studied, not natural. Intelligence performed, not lived.

Vaugh nodded.

"Any idea who?"

Not yet. The mimicry suggests someone near enough to copy her tone, but not close enough to know her syntax.

"Someone in the village, then."

Someone local. Someone who thinks threats need to sound grand.

I studied the edges of the folded paper.

A faint indentation, as if a thumb had pressed too hard along the fold.

Left-handed fold.

Right-handed writer.

Mismatch.

"Whoever wrote this," I murmured, "did not fold it. Those two actions carry different motor patterns."

"So, two people?" Vaugh asked.

"Possibly. Or one person trying to disguise handedness."

I reached for my notebook, jotting down the folding angle, indentation alignment, and ink flow strokes.

The room felt subtly wrong. Someone had left and come back, touching edges, shifting details, but leaving the whole intact. Not staged. Adjusted.

As I worked, Vaugh examined the doorway, where the wood near the latch showed slight splintering. Not enough to break the door entirely. Just enough to weaken it before it was forced. Samuel's "two noises."

"Whoever did this knew exactly where to push," Vaugh said.

"Yes," I said. "Someone familiar with the cottage."

"Or someone strong."

"Strength alone doesn't create targeted damage," I said. "Knowledge does."

His expression shifted in that faint way people do when they don't like the implication but can't refute it.

"I spoke to Eifion Davies last year," Vaugh said. "He did handyman work for half the village. Could've known the structure."

"Possibility," I said.

But Eifion had a limp.

The person in the coat that Samuel saw did not.

A limp changes the way fog gathers around a body. The pattern becomes uneven, broken.

Samuel's fog description was symmetrical.

But I said none of this aloud.

Not yet.

Vaugh approached the bookshelf next. Calendars from previous years were stacked in a pile. Each had tabs marking particular months.

Catrin aligned things. A habit of order.

"What was she tracking?" Vaugh asked.

"Patterns," I said.

"Patterns in what?"

Behaviour. People. Visits. Something she saw but chose not to name.

People often track what they can't yet name."

"And she got close?"

"Yes."

Close enough to unsettle the murderer.

I turned my attention to a second shelf with boxes labelled by year. Inside were parish notices, old receipts, faded photographs of events no one remembered unless they had lived here long enough to understand the weight of them.

A picture caught my attention.

Catrin at a village fete, smiling slightly.

Behind her, Rhian's father, Reverend Lewis, stood with a group of men.

All younger.

All tense.

They stood as people do when they do not want to be photographed but have agreed out of obligation.

A memory, not evidence. Not yet.

I placed it back.

"What else do you see?" Vaugh asked.

"Absence," I said.

"Of what?"

"Her folder?

Vaugh stilled.

"Not here?" he asked.

No. She would not leave it at the school, the shop, or the chapel. Someone took it.

"The murdered."

"Or someone earlier," I said. "Someone who understood its value before Catrin did."

"And the note?" Vaugh asked.

"A replacement," I said. "Something left to obscure the removal."

Vaugh swore softly under his breath.

Outside, a shadow moved past the front window.

We both stilled.

But when Vaugh stepped outside a moment later, the lane was empty.

Fog drifting.

A dog in the distance.

No footsteps.

No figure.

Someone had been watching us.

Someone at home in Bryngwyn, able to move through its fog without sound.

I gathered my notes and stood.

"We have three converging truths," I said.

"Go on."

"One. Catrin was close to understanding something old."

He nodded.

"Two: the person she threatened is afraid of exposure, not conflict."

"And three?"

I closed the notebook.

"Three: the murderer did not expect me."

Vaugh looked at me sharply.

"You think they don't know who you are?"

"I think," I said carefully, "that someone in this village is writing a narrative they believe they can control."

"And they can't," he said.

"No," I said. "Because they do not understand what kind of reader I am."

We stepped out into the lane.

The fog pressed in with gentle insistence.

Somewhere in the village, someone was already reshaping their story to account for me.

It would not be enough.

The narrative was already slipping out of their hands.

Chapter Ten – Edges of Blame

The command room in the chapel hall had expanded by degrees. Paper multiplied across every surface. Tension, too. The air pressed in, dense and expectant, as if the walls were holding their breath.

The map of Bryngwyn bristled with coloured pins. Red marked key locations. Yellow for witness statements. Green for timings that refused to align, no matter how often we rearranged them.

Someone had run a string between a handful of pins. I distrusted string. It implied a pattern but never delivered certainty.

Vaugh placed Samuel's drawing beside the map, aligning the edges. He straightened, movements measured. PC Ellis lingered at the margin, mug in hand, scanning for a task that might justify his presence.

"We need to speak to Eifion," Vaugh said. "Before he rewrites last night entirely."

"Yes," I said, "And Dylan's mention of the dogs suggests he is a necessary data point regardless of motive."

Ellis cleared his throat. "He's at home. I saw his truck outside. The blue one with the broken taillight."

"Has he been told to wait there?" I asked.

"Sergeant Jenkins said not to go wandering off," Ellis replied. "He's not the wandering sort, mind."

"Everyone is the wandering sort when nervous," I said. "They just wander in different directions."

Vaugh pushed back his chair. "Let's go."

He paused by the door. "You want the boy's drawing up here on the board?"

"Yes," I said. "But separate from the map. It has its own geometry."

Ellis pinned it carefully to a clear space, as though aware of the responsibility of exact placement.

Eifion Davies's bungalow was unapologetically seventies—box-shaped, set askew to the lane, as if it had drifted there and stopped. It made an effort to blend with the older stone cottages, but the attempt was half-hearted. The garden was utilitarian: tyres pressed into service as planters, a concrete birdbath, a lawn quietly overtaken by moss.

His dogs announced us before we reached the gate. Two collies, all noise and little certainty, hurled themselves at the low fence, then retreated when they measured Vaugh's height against their courage.

"Morning, Mr Davies," Vaugh called, keeping his voice level. "We'd like a word."

The door opened after a moment.

Eifion stepped out, leaning heavily on a walking stick that had seen as many years as his limp. He was a man built for strength, but his body no longer fully supplied. Broad-shouldered, deep-chested, with lines carved into his face by either laughter or weather. It was hard to tell which.

He looked from Vaugh to me, then to the tape still visible down the lane around Catrin's cottage.

"A word about her, I suppose," he said. "Come in, then. No point pretending I don't know why you're here."

Inside, the sitting room was dense with furniture, not comfort. Framed photographs lined the walls. The television claimed its corner, silent and watchful. A tractor company calendar hung askew, last month's page still visible—a small casualty of disrupted routine.

Eifion eased himself into an armchair. He refused Vaugh's offer of help with a scowl that contained more pride than hostility.

"You want tea?" he asked.

"No, thank you," I said.

"Yes, please," Vaugh replied.

I watched Eifion's face.

Not irritation.

Relief.

He wanted the routine of making tea.

Time to arrange his thoughts.

"Milk, two sugars, if it's not a trouble," Vaugh added.

"Oh, there's always trouble," Eifion said, levering himself back up. "Question is whether it's worth the kettle for it."

He disappeared into the kitchen. Porcelain knocked against porcelain, water ran. The dogs circled, then settled, as if aware this, too, would become part of the story.

"He's rattled," Vaugh muttered.

"Yes," I said. "But not in a way that suggests improvisation. He's rehearsing."

"For us?"

"For what comes after us," I said. "People are already deciding how they'll tell this story at the pub for the next twenty years."

He grimaced. "I'd forgotten that part."

It was the only part some villagers cared about.

Eifion returned with a tray and the slow, careful gait of someone with pain management down to an art. He set the tray on the low table, lowered himself again, and took up his stick like a sceptre.

"Right," he said. "Ask what you're going to ask,"

"We'll start simple," Vaugh said. "Where were you last night between eight and ten?"

"In here," he replied. "Watching telly. There was a quiz show on. Full of idiots, if you ask me.

Answered more questions from this chair than all three contestants together."

"Anyone who can confirm that?" Vaugh asked.

"No," he said. "My wife was over at our daughter's in Aberaeron. I don't need a chaperone to work a remote."

"So, no alibi," Vaugh said.

Eifion's eyes narrowed. "You calling me a liar, Inspector?"

"No," I said calmly. "We're calling you uncorroborated. There's a difference."

He looked at me properly for the first time. Then snorted. "Huh. You're the Cardiff one."

I didn't answer. My location did not affect the facts.

"Your dogs barked around nine," Vaugh said.

"The butcher heard them. Short bark, then quiet. Why??"

"They bark at everything," Eifion said. "Foxes, badgers, shadows, the wind thinking about moving."

"But this time, they stopped quickly," I said. "Samuel Lang noticed it, too."

That caught him off guard. "The boy was out?"

"Yes," I said. "He heard the door to Catrin's. Two noises. Wood and metal."

His jaw tightened.

"The lad hears too much."

"That's rarely a fault," I said.

He looked away.

"Did you go past Catrin's cottage last night?" Vaugh asked.

"No," he said.

"But your dog's saw someone," I said. "Their bark pattern changed. Recognising familiarity, then settled quickly."

He glared. "You get all that from a bark, do you?"

"No," I said. "I get that from people who've lived beside those dogs for years."

His gaze flicked to the window, then back.

"Could've been the Reverend," he muttered. "He walks late sometimes. Or Rhian, coming back from choir practice. Or Dylan heading home. Everyone uses the lane."

"Who are you most comfortable blaming?" I asked.

That earned a sharp bark of laughter. "At least you say it plain."

"Plain speech is efficient," I said.

He leaned back, the chair creaking under his weight.

"Catrin was at the shop last week," he said, unprompted. "Asking daft questions."

"About what?" Vaugh asked.

"Old forms," he said. "Some compensation nonsense from years back. Said some dates didn't line up. I told her dates never line up. Clocks don't ask permission from people."

"You were involved in those forms?" I asked.

He scratched his chin. "My father was. Lost part of his leg in that mess years ago. Paperwork went on for months. Council arguing, company arguing, church keeping quiet. None of it brought his leg back."

His tone flattened on the last sentence.

Not self-pity.

Weariness.

"And did Catrin know that?" I asked.

"Everyone knows that" he said. "Not a secret."

"But she knew details," I said.

He hesitated.

"She knew someone had signed off on an inspection that never really happened," he admitted. "Said she saw the signature in two different places, same date, miles apart. She thought it was important."

"And you didn't?" I asked.

"I thought it was twenty-odd years too late," he said. "Dead men don't change their stories."

"But living people do," I said.

His gaze snapped to mine.

He didn't like that.

"She wouldn't let it alone," he went on. "Said if the village wanted to pretend certain things, that was fine, but the records shouldn't lie. Records should tell the truth."

"And you disagreed?" I asked.

"I said records don't have to live with the consequences," he said.

Silence settled between us.

"Did you threaten her?" Vaugh asked.

"No," he said. "I told her she was going to upset people who'd already spent their lives being upset once. I told her to leave it."

"It?" I repeated.

He shrugged. "All of it. The forms, the notices, the names carved where they maybe shouldn't have been carved."

The chapel plaque.

Names absent.

Names elsewhere.

"And she ignored you," I said.

"Yes," he said simply. "She said, 'The truth doesn't vanish because we stop looking at it, Eifion.'"

Vaugh scribbled something in his notebook.

"You argued?" he asked.

"No," Eifion said. "I don't argue with women holding that much determination—waste of breath. I just told her to be careful what she pulled on. You tug the wrong thread, and the whole jumper comes apart."

"And you think she tugged the wrong thread?" I asked.

"I think," he said, staring at the dogs now, "That she found a thread someone else didn't even know was loose, and they panicked."

"Not you?" I said.

"No," he said flatly. "I stopped panicking about that lot years ago. Nothing left to lose there."

His leg, his father, the past. Yes.

"Where were you working, back there?" I asked.

He gave me a sideways look. "Up near the old footpath. Before the bodies were brought down."

"Is there anything else we should know?" Vaugh asked.

"Yes," Eifion said after a brief pause. "Catrin was holding something back."

Vaugh frowned. "What do you mean?"

"She came by two weeks ago with that folder of hers," he said. "Blue thing. Thick. Asked me to confirm the order of some events. I corrected her on one date. She didn't write it down."

"Why not?" I asked.

"She said, 'I only needed to see how you'd say it.'" He shook his head, "She already had it right. She just wanted to watch me lie before I corrected myself."

A quiet respect coloured his voice now. It surprised him more than us.

"She was testing your version against her own," I said.

"Yes."

"And that frightened you?" I asked.

He considered. "Didn't frighten me. Just reminded me we don't always get away with what we think we've buried."

"And whoever killed her?" I said. "Do you think they're   frightened?"

"I think they were," he said. "Last night. Right up until they hit her. After that, I don't know what they are."

We left with more information, but nothing that closed any gaps. Bryngwyn was a village of people who had struck bargains with the past and now waited for the bill to arrive.

Outside, the dogs barked again as we reached the gate.

Short burst.

Then silence.

"Familiar pattern," I said.

"They don't like uniforms," Vaugh replied.

"No," I said. "They don't like disruption."

He adjusted his coat as we walked back toward the village centre.

"Well?" he asked.

"Well," I echoed. "We have a man with motive, no alibi, a dislike of Catrin's questions, and proximity."

"But?" he prompted.

"But his fear is old," I said. "Stale. There's no freshness in it."

"And we're looking for fresh fear," he said.

"Yes," I said. "The kind that leaves a note trying to sound clever."

We were nearly at the crossroads when an unfamiliar car crept into the village. Silver hatchback, hire company stickers ghosting the windscreen. The driver's eyes moved from building to building, following a script only she could see.

"Outsider," Vaugh muttered.

The car stopped near the post office. A woman stepped out—city coat, city shoes, folder in hand. She paused, taking her bearings, then set off toward the shop with a kind of practiced resolve.

"Who's that??" I asked.

"Not local," Vaugh said. "You can tell from the way she's trying not to stare."

I watched her for a moment.

New data.

New variables.

"Think she's connected?" Vaugh asked.

"Everything here is connected," I said. "The question is how obviously."

We turned toward the chapel.

The memorial plaque caught my eye again.

A year.

No Names.

Truth makes cowards of the unprepared, the note had said.

Bryngwyn had lived with half-truths so long they had acquired the weight of fact.

Someone, somewhere, had realised they were about to be read for what they were.

And they were not ready.

Chapter Eleven – A Visitor With an Old Map

The outsider stood at the post office counter; voice lowered in the way city people do when they sense the rules have changed. Mrs Pritchard lingered behind the till, her face a careful arrangement of curiosity and suspicion, with a civility sharp enough to be saved for later use.

Vaugh and I stepped inside. The bell above the door gave its brittle chime, a sound that always seemed too fragile for the room. The woman turned.

Tall, late thirties perhaps, red hair pinned in a flat bun, sharp-edged glasses. Her shoes were wrong for Bryngwyn: suede, impractical, already losing the battle to the village damp. She clutched a leather satchel close to her side, as though guarding its contents from the very air.

"Inspector?" she asked.

A city accent, Cardiff in the vowels, the rhythm shaped by years of lectures and libraries.

Vaugh approached her first. "That depends," he said. "Who are you?"

She produced an ID wallet in a swift, practised motion.

Carys Morgan

Senior Records Analyst

Ceredigion Council

Not police.

Not a detective.

A paper person.

I stepped closer. "Records analyst for which branch?"

She hesitated. Not uncertain. Calculating.

"We cover legacy holdings," she said. "Archival material relating to land use, parish structures, employment injuries, compensation boards — the things that people forget until they don't. "

"And old inspection reports," I finished.

The flicker in her eyes confirmed it.

Mrs Pritchard, barely containing her delight, rearranged envelopes with the focus of someone who would recount every word to her sister before the kettle boiled.

"We weren't expecting a council representative," Vaugh said.

"You didn't request one," Carys replied. "But we received a message indicating a resident had recently accessed certain protected records."

She paused. "Here."

Something in me shifted, quietly, as if a line had been drawn and I'd only just noticed.

Not enough to call it certainty.

Just enough to mark the moment for later.

"What records?" Vaugh asked.

She reached into her satchel and pulled out a slim folder in a waterproof sleeve.

Borrowed documents. Logged out six days ago.

"And by 'removed,' you mean?" Vaugh said.

She folded her hands. "Visited. Photographed. Handwritten notes taken."

"By whom?" Vaugh asked.

Her hesitation was brief.

Measured.

"By the deceased," she said.

Catrin.

Of course.

"What did she look at?" I asked, hoping her answer would be small, manageable, ordinary.

"It wasn't.

"A sequence of forms," she said softly. "From 1992. Council-led review. Joint signatories from the parish and the oversight committee."

Her gaze flicked, briefly, to the chapel door. "It was a difficult year."

"And?" Vaugh prompted.

Her fingers tensed slightly on the sleeve.

"And one of the signature pages was.... Irregular."

Irregular. The word people reach for when they can't—or won't—say fraudulent.

"Explain," I said.

She opened the folder and slid a photocopy across the counter.

Three signatures.

Three dates.

All neatly aligned.

Except —

"The same person signed twice," I said.

She nodded.

"And on two different committees on the same day."

"And the third signature?" I asked.

"Never authenticated."

"Meaning?" Vaugh said.

"Meaning," she continued carefully, "the record stood because no one questioned it. The assumption was clerical oversight or inconvenience in obtaining second signatures."

"And Catrin – questioned it," I said.

"She emailed twice," Carys murmured. "Requesting clarification."

A fractional pause.

"A third email never arrived."

A coldness settled between my ribs, quiet and precise.

"When you say 'protected,'" I asked, "what do you mean? Legally protected? Or socially?"

Carys looked over her glasses, as though checking the room for eavesdroppers.

"Both," Carys said. "Legally first."

Then, quieter. "Socially always."

"And why come here personally?" Vaugh asked.

Her gaze shifted to the window, where fog pressed its patterns against the glass, as if trying to read the room from outside.

"Because I received a second message," she said. "Anonymous. Sent early this morning."

"And because I didn't want it... handled internally."

Vaugh stiffened. "From whom?"

She slid another page out of the satchel.

A printed email.

STOP SENDING INFORMATION TO BRYNGWYN.

YOU'RE MAKING A MISTAKE YOU WON'T BE ABLE TO UNDO.

No sign-off.

No punctuation.

The tone was fraught but controlled.

"This arrived at 6:14 AM," she said. "And I decided I couldn't ignore it."

I read the lines twice, then once more, this time analysing structure.

The pronouns.

The cadence.

The missing punctuation.

The tense choices.

"Not written by the same author as the note found at the cottage," I said.

"Different person entirely."

"Are you certain?" Carys asked.

"Yes," I said. "This person isn't imitating decorum. They're attempting restraint. Very poorly.
What does that tell you?" Vaugh asked.

"That the writer is frightened," I said. "Not angry. Fear is quieter than anger."

Carys swallowed. "So, someone in this village doesn't want these records re-examined."

"Again."

"No," I corrected gently. "Someone in the village didn't want them examined again by Catrin."

Mrs Pritchard froze mid-rearrangement of envelopes.

Vaugh leaned in. "Do you know who might have had access to these forms back then?"

"Yes," Carys said. "A short list. But one signature appears across multiple unrelated reports. Someone very involved."

"And that person is-?"

She hesitated.

Not uncertainty. Dread.

"Reverend Lewis," she said softly. "Your retired parish chair before Reverend Thomas took over."

Rhian's father.

Of course.

Not guilt.

But origin.

"Was he known to Catrin?" Vaugh asked.

"Yes," Carys said. "And to half the village. But the records don't tell us if his signature was legitimate or delegated."

"He had authority," I said. "Authority invites assumption.:

"And assumption invites misuse," she replied quietly.

The room tilted, not in any physical sense, but as if the story itself had changed direction.

"So Catrin found inconsistencies," Vaugh said. "And someone panicked."

"Possibly several someone's," I added.

Carys closed her satchel slowly, the movement deliberate, as if to avoid making noise that might carry beyond the post office walls.

"I need you to understand," she said, her voice low. "I didn't come to accuse anyone. I came because a woman is dead, and whatever she found shouldn't die with her."

A beat.

"We've lost enough to silence."

Her sincerity was real.

Her fear was also real.

Fear of being entangled in a village's old secret.

"And what do you expect us to do?" Vaugh asked gently.

"Tell the truth," She whispered. "Even if Bryngwyn won't.

Outside, a single bark cut through the fog—a sharp sound, then silence, as if the air itself had swallowed it.

We all turned toward the door.

A shape had passed the window.

Too fast.

Too silent.

A coat.

Long.

Dark.

My pulse found a new rhythm, uneasy and quick.

"Inspector?" Carys whispered.

"I saw it," I said.

But the lane was empty when Vaugh stepped outside.

Fog only moves when something disturbs it.

Samuel had said so.

And he was right.

Someone was listening.

Watching.

Recalibrating.

Bryngwyn was no longer a village sidestepping its past.

It was a village beginning to realise the past had started to name its price.

And someone.

Someone who feared losing everything.

Was preparing to pay with more than silence.

Chapter Twelve – A Crack in the Quiet

By mid-afternoon, the fog had receded to a thin veil. Moisture clung to the chapel steps, darkening the stone in irregular patches where boots had passed. A cluster of villagers remained at the edge of the square, their voices low, the cadence of their conversation more revealing than the words themselves.

Inside the temporary incident room, the air was thick with instant coffee, printer toner, and the kind of impatience that accumulates in silence.

I stood before the evidence board, reading it the way I would read a sentence that contained a grammatical error. The error was small, so small that most readers would pass over it without noticing. But once seen, it refused to be unseen.

"Something's wrong with the timeline," I said.

Vaugh, who had been finishing a phone call, turned. "Which part?"

"All of it," I said. "But one piece doesn't align at all."

I tapped a yellow pin marking the butcher's shop.

"Dylan saw Catrin at four twenty-three," I said. "He's precise about time because he sets his counter alarm for deliveries. His watch matches the shop's digital clock. That gives us a confirmed timestamp."

"And Eifion saw her soon after," Vaugh said.

"No," I corrected. "He says he saw her 'heading down the land,' but he never specifies the time. He lets us assume it's shortly after Dylan's sighting."

Vaugh frowned. "But that's what makes sense."

"Sense," I said, "is not the same as truth."

He crossed to the board, studying the pins more closely now.

"So, what are you saying? Eifion lied?"

"Not lied," I said. "Rearranged."

The distinction was slight, but it mattered. Some lied to mislead; others, to shield themselves from scrutiny. In Bryngwyn, the second was almost a local tradition.

"Why would he shift the time?" Vaugh asked.

"To distance himself," I said. "From a moment he doesn't want associated with him."

"But that doesn't make him a murderer."

"No," I said. "It makes him someone who fears implication."

Vaugh rubbed the bridge of his nose. "All right. What else doesn't fit?"

I shifted to the next set of notes: Mrs Pritchard's account, the Reverend's memory, Rhian's recollection of Catrin earlier that week.

"The Reverend," I said. "He claims Catrin came by last Tuesday. But Rhian says he never mentioned it at home."

"Could be an oversight," Vaugh said.

"He remembers fine detail about squirrel tracks in his garden," I replied. "People don't forget visits that disturb them."

"You think Catrin disturbed him?"

"Yes," I said, "but she disturbed him because she asked a question he felt unprepared to answer.

"And Rhian?" Vaugh asked, "You've been quiet about her."

I paused.

Rhian's posture: diminished, apologetic in the absence of any offence. Her gaze flickered to the chapel each time 1992 surfaced in conversation. It was not guilt I saw.

It was the residue of someone who had lived beside guilt for years, breathing it in until it settled beneath the skin.

"She's withholding something," I said. "But I don't believe it's violent."

"Then what?"

"A memory," I said. "A single memory with sharp edges."

Vaugh exhaled.

"Anyone else standing out?" he asked.

"Yes," I said. "The person in the coat."

"The one Samuel say?"

"Yes. And the one who passed the post office today, while we were speaking with Carys."

"You think it's the same person?"

"Yes," I said simply. "People have unique ways of entering fog. They leave different shapes."

He blinked. "I'll take your word for it.:

"You should," I said. "Fog reveals more than it hides."

He opened his mouth to reply, but the chapel door creaked.

Sergeant Jenkins stepped inside, cheeks flushed.

"Sir – Mr Davies asked if the police could stop by later," he said. "He said he might have remembered something about yesterday."

Vaugh Straightened. "Something useful?"

"He didn't say. Only that it was 'better mentioned than left.'"

I noted that phrasing.

Eifion rarely used moral language unless pushed.

"Did he sound distressed?" I asked.

Jenkins hesitated. "Not distressed. Cautious. Like he wanted to say something but wasn't sure if he should."

That was an interesting inversion.

Earlier, he had been sure of what not to say.

"We'll head there in a bit," Vaugh said. "As soon as we finish here."

"Sir," Jenkins said. "One more thing. His dogs won't settle today. Neighbours complained."

This was predictable. Animals register emotional disturbance before humans articulate it. Still, it lent weight to the pattern assembling itself in my mind.

"Thank you, Sergeant," I said.

She nodded and left.

Vaugh turned back to me. "Well?"

"Well," I said, "someone visited Eifion last night?"

"You're sure?"

"Yes."

This was not conjecture. It was a deduction grounded in behaviour.

"And that visit unsettled him."

"Yes," I said. "People rearrange timelines when they feel watched."

 He blew out a sign. "And the coat? Whoever that was?"

"Possibly the same visitor," I said. "But we cannot confirm."

Silence settled over the chapel, dense and deliberate.

"Pryce," Vaugh said suddenly, "does this... feel like the kind of case where someone kills once and stops?"

"No," I said quietly. "It feels like the kind of case where someone kills to delay something inevitable."

"And when the delay fails?"

"They kill again."

He nodded once, sharply.

Recognition, not fear.

But his eyes darkened.

"Then we'd better get to Eifion," he said.

"Before he changes his mind."

We stepped into the lane. The fog had collapsed into a pale ribbon, trailing low along the verge.

Somewhere nearby, a dog barked—once, then again.

A brief pattern.

Then silence.

Not the dogs.

Eifion's dogs.

I stopped.

"Pryce?" Vaugh asked.

"That bark was wrong," I said.

"What do you mean by 'wrong'?

"Wrong for the afternoon," I said. "Wrong for greeting. Wrong for warning."

He stiffened. "You think…?"

"I think," I said carefully, "that the dogs recognise someone. But not with comfort."

We quickened our pace.

As we turned toward the crossroads, the wind shifted and carried something faint—wooden rattling, like a loose latch.

A reflexive part of my mind tried to classify the sound.

My conscious mind interrupted immediately.

It was not a latch.

Not wood.

It was the sound of a door hitting a frame with no one left to close it.

Eifion's door.

We began to run.

Chapter Thirteen – A Fall That Didn't Happen

We reached Eifion's bungalow faster than I liked. Running disrupted observation; it forced the world into a blur when I needed it in focus.

The dogs met us at the fence, barking with frantic urgency this time. No short burst. No quick settling. They crashed against the gate, nails scrabbling on concrete, bodies in full alarm.

"Something's wrong," Vaugh said unnecessarily.

The front curtains were open. The light inside was on. The door was closed but not latched properly. The frame sat slightly off, as if the house had inhaled and forgotten to exhale.

"Mr Davies?" Vaugh called, pushing the gate. It resisted, caught on mud ridged under its swing. He shoved harder. It gave way.

The dogs surged forward, then stopped dead as we approached the door, as if an invisible line held them back. Their hackles rose. One whined, a keening sound that seemed too fragile for their size.

"Stay," I said.

They did.

Not because they understood the word, but because something in the air told them crossing the threshold was a bad idea.

Vaugh rapped on the door. "Eifion? It's Inspector Vaugh. We're coming in."

No response.

Only the sound of the wind catching the old footpath sign down the lane—a faint wooden creak, like an exhausted hinge remembering its purpose.

Vaugh pushed the door. It opened with reluctant ease, as if it had been expecting us but not welcoming us.

"Police!" he called, "Mr Davies?"

The hallway smelled faintly of fried onions and the metallic tang of boiler water. The living room door stood open on the left. The television muttered to itself, volume low, some quiz show where strangers guessed answers to questions no one would remember.

"Stay here," Vaugh said over his shoulder.

"No," I replied, and stepped in beside him.

The sitting room was empty, with cushions slightly compressed where someone had recently sat. A mug of tea on the side table still showed steam barely rising. Not long.

"Back door," I said.

The kitchen was small, neat in a practical way. A pan sat on the hob, cleaned but not dried. A second walking stick leaned against the wall — his spare — and a third, older one lay abandoned near the back door, as if it had been knocked aside.

The back door stood ajar. Not wide. Just enough for air to slip in and out. The latch hung at an odd angle, as if arguing with the frame.

Vaugh moved forward carefully and pushed the door open with two fingers.

I saw the steps before I saw Eifion.

Three concrete steps led down to a narrow yard behind the house. Moss and algae traced the edges, lending the surfaces a false promise of stability.

At the foot of the steps, Eifion Davies lay on his side, head twisted at a degree that the human neck does not tolerate. One arm bent under him at an impossible angle, his stick just beyond the reach of his hand.

At first glance, the arrangement implied accident.

The angles, though, resisted that reading.

'Stay back," Vaugh said sharply.

"I am back," I said. "Relatively."

He shot me a look that would have been exasperation under other circumstances.

"Ambulance," he said. "Though it's too late."

He stepped out into the yard with measured care and bent to check for a pulse out of procedure rather than hope. After a moment, he straightened, jaw tight.

"Time of death?" I asked.

"We'll know more later,' he said. "He's cold, but not long."

My gaze moved slowly, deliberately.

A small pool of blood beneath his head, not enough for violence. His shirt, untucked on one side, suggested a hand had found it. His boots rested on separate steps—one on the second, one on the third. The arrangement refused the logic of a simple fall.

"Look at his feet," I said.

"What about them?" Vaugh asked.

"Eifion descends stairs with his right foot first," I said. "He favours his left leg. He demonstrated it earlier without realising."

"This could be different," Vaugh said. "He could have slipped."

"Slipping doesn't reverse habit," I said. "His right foot is higher. This implies he was moved, not fell."

Vaugh stared at the stair arrangement, recalibrating.

"You're sure?" he asked.

"Yes," I said.

"Don't answer so fast."

"I'm not answering fast," I said. I'm answering accurately. There's a difference."

I moved a fraction closer, staying clear of the body, letting my attention slide over the peripheral details instead: the doorframe, the latch, the threshold.

Mud marked the inner edge of the threshold. Not much—just enough to register if you were inclined to look for it.

"Those are not his footprints," I said.

"Because?" Vaugh asked.

"He drags his left foot slightly," I said. "Leave a scuff, not a clean tread. These are symmetrical."

He muttered a quiet curse.

"Someone came in," I said. "Someone who doesn't limp. And then someone left."

"Who? When?" he asked.

"The dogs barked," I said. "Short pattern. Twice today. Once last night. Each time followed by immediate quiet."

"Someone they recognised," he said.

"Yes," I said. "And someone they associate with authority, not threat."

His expression shifted. "You think it's the Reverend?"

"Possibly," I said. "Or Rhian. Or Dylan. Or anyone whose presence here had been normalised."

"Could it be a stranger?" he asked.

"No," I said. "Strangers leave different silences."

He stared at me. "I'll take your word for that."

"You should," I said.

He exhaled. "If this is murder, it's a good imitation of an accident."

"Yes," I said. "Because the murderer understands how accidents work here. Bryngwyn is well-practised at them."

The back door shifted slightly in the breeze. The latch tapped against the frame with a small, repetitive sound.

"See that?" I said.

"The latch?" he asked.

"It's bent inward," I said. "As if forced from outside when shut. Not simply old. Recent force."

'You're saying whoever came to his back door had to persuade it to open."

"Yes," I said. "And Eifion wouldn't have been careless with it in this weather. He told his dogs off for less."

I stepped back, letting my gaze settle on the yard's arrangement. The bins stood in their usual order. Wellington boots by the shed, upright, undisturbed. A plastic chair leaned against the wall, its legs damp on one side, as if it had been shifted and returned without much thought.

Vaugh followed my gaze. "What?"

"He doesn't sit," I said. "He braces."

"You got that from one visit?" he asked.

"Yes," I said. "He lowers himself carefully. A plastic chair is dangerous for someone with his balance. He wouldn't risk it."

"Then why is it out?" Vaugh asked.

"To give the person at the door somewhere to wait," I said. "They expected a conversation, not an argument."

A conversation, interrupted at the foot of the steps.

Vaugh called in the discovery. Officers began to arrive with the grim efficiency of people who had done this before and never hoped to again.

Sergeant Jenkins moved toward the back door, expression shuttered.

"Neighbours heard anything?" Vaugh asked.

"One said she heard voices about half an hour ago," Jenkins said. "Didn't catch words. Just tone. Male and female."

"Arguing?" I asked.

"Not exactly. More like one trying to convince the other of something they didn't want," Jenkins said.

The model sharpened in my mind.

"Did she recognise the voices?" I asked.

"Not enough to swear to it," Jenkins said. "But she said one 'sounded like school'."

"Like school?" Vaugh repeated.

"Her exact phrase," Jenkins said. "I wrote it down."

We already knew what she meant.

"Rhian," Vaugh said under his breath.

"Or another teacher," I said. "Or anyone who uses that same tone with children"

"Or with someone they think needs managing," he muttered.

The paramedics left as quietly as they had arrived, their work more ceremonial than functional now. Two officers moved to secure the backyard, their faces taut.

The dogs whined at the fence, restless, confused. I stepped toward them, keeping my hands to myself. They sniffed the air obsessively, eyes flicking toward the house as if waiting for Eifion to reappear and correct this error.

"He won't come out," I said softly.

One of them gave a small, uncertain bark.

Not alarm.

Loss.

"Pryce," Vaugh called.

I turned.

He'd stepped back inside; the silhouette of his shoulders framed against the hallway light.

"There's something in his sitting room you should see.'

The living room had contracted, the air thickened by absence. The television was silent now. The quiz show's contestants left without witnesses.

On the coffee table lay a notebook. Not the tractor calendar, not council forms. Just a cheap spiral-bound pad, with the edges slightly curled.

"He had been writing, Vaugh said.

I approached.

The handwriting was large, uneven, formed by a hand not used to extended script. He had printed, not written in joined-up letters.

I read the last page.

THEN WE ALL SIGNED WRONG

RH SAID IT DIDN'T MATTER

BUT IT DOES

IT MATTERED TO MY DAD

IT MATTERED TO THE ONES WHO DIED

IF THEY FIND OUT I KNEW, THEY'LL THINK I

The sentence stopped mid-line.

My gaze fixed on the line above.

RH SAID IT DIDN'T MATTER

"RH?" Vaugh asked over my shoulder.

"Reverend Hughes?"

"No," I said quietly. "He always refers to him as 'Lewis' or 'the old one'. No initials."

"Then who?" Vaugh asked.

"Rhian," I said.

The name lingered, heavy in the room.

"She was a child then," Vaugh said.

"Yes," I said. "But children see things. And adults tell them stories they shouldn't have to carry."

He rubbed the back of his neck. "If she knew, why hide it?"

"The same reason as the others," I said. "The story was necessary. Breaking it would have cost too much."

He looked at the unfinished sentence again.

"Do you think the murdered knew he'd written this?" he asked.

"No," I said. "If they had, the notebook wouldn't be here."

"Then why kill him now?" he asked.

"Because he was about to talk," I said. "He'd asked for us. That alone was enough to frighten someone who's survived this long on silence."

Vaugh lowered himself into an armchair, then stood again, unsettled by the furniture's silent witness.

"This changes everything," he said.

"It confirms everything," I corrected. "We already knew someone would kill again."

He looked at me. "You really don't sugar-coat anything, do you?"

"It's an inefficient use of time," I said.

He huffed something like a laugh, then stopped, the sound aborted.

"What now?" he asked.

"Now," I said, "we stop treating Catrin's murder as an isolated event and start treating these deaths as what they are."

"And what's that?" he asked.

"A delayed consequence," I said. "The past has reached its limit of being ignored."

"A delayed consequence," I said. "The past has reached its limit of being ignored."

I looked out the window. Villagers had begun to gather, careful in their distance. News moved faster than any official word, faster than sense.

Two deaths now.

Two people tangled in the old records Catrin had tried to align.

Somewhere in Bryngwyn, someone in a long coat had chosen to send an old man down the steps rather than answer a question left unspoken for decades.

They believed they could still shape the narrative.

They had not yet learned that some stories, once set in motion, demand their own ending.

Chapter Fourteen – A Village Rearranges Itself

News of Eifion's death threaded through Bryngwyn, silent and certain as smoke drawn to a crack in the window. When Vaugh and I stepped outside, the village had already shifted its shape. Curtains hung at uneasy angles. People hovered in doorways, brooms in hand, flowerpots nudged a fraction to the left—each gesture a cover for watching.

Mrs Pritchard advanced up the lane, apron knotted, arms folded across her chest. The gesture was less protection than warning.

"Is it true?" she demanded before we reached her, "Tell me it's not true."

Vaugh hesitated.

She misinterpreted it correctly.

"Oh God." Her hands rose to her mouth. "Not Eifion. Not him?"

Behind her, Dylan emerged from the butcher's shop, apron stained from the morning's work.

His expression darkened when he caught sight of Vaugh's face.

"No," he muttered. "Not him as well."

His words landed heavy, the sound of someone who had learned there are wounds no blade can mend.

Mrs Pritchard's voice rose. "What happened? Was he attacked? Was it an accident? What are we meant to think?"

"That you should go home," Vaugh said gently. "We'll speak with everyone once we've confirmed the circumstances."

She didn't move.

She stared at Vaugh with sharp, searching eyes.

"Is this about Catrin was looking into?"

A ripple moved through the cluster of villagers behind her. Fear. Recognition. Eyes sliding away.

"Mrs Pritchard," Vaugh said, "go home."

At last, she did.

Dylan waited until she'd gone before speaking. "Tell me straight. This wasn't a fall, was it?"

Vaugh didn't answer.

It was an answer enough.

Dylan swore under his breath, a quiet, defeated sound.

He wiped his hands on his apron, as if the gesture could erase something that clung beneath the skin.

"This place," he muttered. "It's happening again."

I paused. "Again?"

He realised his misstep too late.

His jaw tightened.

"Forget I said anything."

"I can't," I said simply.

He looked at me, hollow-eyed, then retreated into the shop. The door closed with a sound that ended the conversation, but not the story.

Rhian Lewis lived two doors from the chapel, in a cottage with window frames the colour of new leaves. Hydrangeas crowded the front garden, petals browning at the edges, surrendering to autumn. The air carried a trace of baking—burnt sugar, lemon. The scent felt out of place.

We knocked.

It took a long time for her to answer. Long enough that Vaugh shifted from foot to foot.

When she opened the door, her face was pale, eyes reddened.

She had been crying.

Recently.

"Rhian," Vaugh said softly. "May we come in?"

She stepped aside automatically, as though her body responded before her mind had fully registered the request.

The sitting room was small, every surface ordered. Books by size, cushions squared, a blanket folded with the precision of a parade ground. A mug rested on the table, tea untouched, the steam already vanished.

"I saw people running down the lane," she said, voice trembling. "And then I heard. I heard them say."

She stopped.

Vaugh's expression softened.

"I'm sorry," he said. "It's true. Eifion's died."

Her hands flew to her mouth. She sank onto the sofa, looking suddenly much younger than her thirty-something years.

"I saw him yesterday," she whispered. "He waved at me."

"When?" I asked.

"After school. About half past four. Maybe a bit later."

That made four people who had fixed Catrin's last afternoon in place.

The pattern grew clearer with each account.

"He was in his garden," she continued. "He said he'd been meaning to stop by the school. I thought he wanted to talk about the children's project. He didn't seem... frightened."

"He didn't," I said.

"But he called you," Vaugh added. "Earlier. Said he'd remembered something."

Rhian nodded faintly.

"He told me last week that I should leave...old questions alone. But he wasn't angry. Just tired. He always said he didn't like thinking backwards."

Her voice faltered.

"And now he's gone," she whispered. "Just like that. First Catrin. Now Eifion. Something is wrong here."

"Yes," I said. "There is."

She looked up, eyes sharp. Fear and recognition flickered there.

"What do you know?" she asked.

Not defensively.

Desperately.

"That people are beginning to react," I said.

'To old events resurfacing. And to new danger."

She clasped her hands tightly, knuckles whitening.

"My father," she said suddenly. "Have you spoken to him today?"

Vaugh and I exchanged a glance.

"No," Vaugh said. "Should we?"

She shook her head, the movement too quick.

"I don't know," she whispered. "He's been strange since Catrin died. Quieter. He takes long walks and comes back pale. Yesterday he-"She stopped herself, pressing a fist to her mouth.

'Rhian," Vaugh asked gently, "what happened yesterday?"

"He came home late," she whispered. "And he wouldn't tell me where he's been."

Her breathing quickened.

"And when I said Eifion had looked upset earlier in the week, he said – he said- "

She broke off, burying her face in her hands.

Vaugh moved closer. "He said what?"

Her voice emerged in a fractured whisper.

"He said, 'Some people are better off gone than stirring up trouble.'"

A long silence settled.

She shook her head violently. "He didn't mean it like that. He'd never hurt anyone. He's just tired. And scared. Everyone is scared."

"No one is accusing him," I said softly. "Not yet."

She looked at me. Searching, pleading.

"But he's not the only one acting strangely, is he??" she whispered. "People are changing. Like the whole village is holding its breath."

"Yes," I said. "People under pressure adjust their behaviour. Sometimes subtly. Sometimes dramatically."

"Does that mean someone is going to die again?" she asked, voice breaking.

"Not if we can prevent it," Vaugh said firmly.

She pressed a shaking hand to her forehead. "I don't understand. Catrin wasn't – she wasn't doing anything wrong. And Eifion. He was just trying to protect. Protect something."

"Protect what?" I asked.

She hesitated too long.

"Rhian," Vaugh said, "what was he trying to protect?"

She stared at the hydrangeas outside the window.

Her voice thinned to a thread.

"His fathers. And mine. And others," she whispered. "They made a decision years ago. They thought they were doing the right thing."

"And were they?" I asked.

She shook her head.

A small, splintered motion.

"Maybe once," she whispered. "But not anymore."

Her eyes filled again.

"The village made itself small," she said. "Small enough to forget. But Catrin made it big again. Too big."

Her shoulders shook, barely.

"And now she's dead. Eifion too. I'm scared someone else will be next."

"Who?" I asked.

She swallowed hard.

"You," she whispered.

The walk back to the chapel was silent.

Fog pressed against the cottages, low and restless, moving as if it had intent.

A door slammed somewhere out of sight. Vaugh and I both turned, alert.

"She's scared for you," he said.

"Yes," I said.

"Are you scared for you?" he asked.

"No," I said. "But I am aware."

He eyed me.

"You're being targeted."

"Yes," I said. "Because I don't belong here. The murderer believes that makes me the least predictable variable."

"And does it?" he asked.

"No," I said. "It makes me the most."

He frowned. "Explain that."

"I see the village differently," I said. "People who grew up here look at Bryngwyn like a memory. I look at it like evidence."

"And evidence doesn't lie." Vaugh said.

"No," I said. "But people do. Especially when they believe their survival depends on it."

We reached the chapel steps. The memorial stone waited on the wall—unmarked, unadorned, catching what little light there was.

A date.

No names.

A silence pressed into stone.

Vaugh stared at the stone. "Do you think all this goes back to whatever happened then?"

"No," I said. "It goes back to what people decided to do after."

"And what was that?" he asked.

"To pretend a tragedy was smaller than it was."

"And now?"

"Now," I said, "the tragedy bites back."

We stepped into the chapel, the door shutting behind us with a muted thud.

Somewhere outside, a long coat shifted through fog.

Someone, unseen, was watching the chapel window.

And the story they tried to hold was already slipping away.

Chapter Fifteen – The Shape of a Lie

By early evening, the chapel's acoustics had thickened, as if the walls were hoarding the residue of every conversation, each one layering over the last. The map of Bryngwyn on the table was dense with pins, their arrangement more anxious than orderly. The paper's edges curled upward, as if recoiling from the weight of what had been pinned to it.

Vaugh lingered by the coffee table, coaxing a thin stream of tea from a pot whose best days were a memory. The liquid was the colour of old brass, more suggestion than substance.

"You're staring at that board like it personally offended you," he said

"It has," I said. "It insists on presenting data in an illogical order."

"That's us," he said, "Not the board."

"Yes," I said, "That offends me as well."

He snorted, then sobered.

"So," he said. "You said something earlier about 'rearranging truths. Care to translate that into something useful?"

"I am translating it," I said. "It simply takes longer than you'd like."

I moved a step closer to the board.

The yellow pins marked *statements*.

The red: *locations*.

The green: *times*.

It presented itself as neat. It was not. The order was only surface-deep, a fiction maintained by colour and geometry.

"People don't lie in tidy blocks," I said. "They lie in smudges,"

"Poetic," he said. "Which smudge do you like least?"

"Rhian's," I said.

He stiffened. "You think she-?"

"I think she made a mistake," I said. "Not about murder. About chronology."

I tapped the note pinned near her name.

"Yesterday she told us she saw Eifion at 'half past four, maybe a bit later,' in his garden, "I said. "That fit comfortably into our existing timeline, so we accepted it."

"And now?" he asked.

"Now," I said. "I've looked at her attendance records."

He blinked. "You went through school records?"

"Yes," I said. "You were on the phone. It was a productive use of the hold music."

I lifted a photocopy from the table and held it out to him.

"Yesterday," I continued, "she had an after-school club. A literacy group. It's logged as running until sixteen forty-five. She initialled it herself."

He scanned the sheet. 'So, she couldn't have been walking past Eifion's at half four."

"No," I said. "Not unless she's discovered how to bilocate."

"She could have rounded the time," he said.

"People do that."

"She doesn't," I said. We have records for three other days. She notes late pickups to the minute. Her sense of time is precise in professional contexts."

"So why soften it here?" he asked.

"To distance herself from something," I said.

"Again."

"Same as Eifion?" he asked.

"Yes. But for a different reason."

He stared at the sheet again.

"You think she didn't see him then at all?"

"No," I said. "I think she saw him later."

"When?"

"After five," I said. "Possibly closer to six."

"That's a big difference," he said.

"Not emotionally,' I replied. "But for a murder inquiry, yes."

He rubbed his forehead. "And why would she shift it earlier?"

"To make it line up with a safer version of events," I said. "Where she passes a man in his garden while the village is still busy, rather than later, when it's quiet, and movements are more noticeable."

"Guilt?" he asked.

"Fear," I said. "Not the same thing."

He dropped the sheet on the table.

"All right," he said. "That's one contradiction. Any others?"

"Yes," I said. "The Reverend."

He groaned quietly. "Of course."

"His statement about last night," I said. "He said he was indoors, preparing his sermon, a 'quiet night'."

"Yes."

"Carys's arrival this morning disturbed him," I said. "But that's not the important part."

I picked up another sheet: Sergeant Jenkins' log from their morning canvass.

"She asked him, out of habit, if he'd been out walking when he heard about Catrin," I said. "He said, 'I walk most evenings. Last night I didn't go as far as usual."

Vaugh frowned. "He told us he stayed in all evening."

"Yes," I said, "Chronology smudged again."

"You think he's covering for being near Catrin's cottage?" Vaugh asked.

"No," I said, "If he were, he would be more careful."

"Then what's he covering?"

"Who he spoke to," I said.

The realisation arrived, compact and heavy, settling in the space between us.

"You think he saw someone?" Vaugh asked.

"Yes," I said. "And he doesn't want us asking who."

He paced, slow and measured.

"All right," he said. "So, Rhian misplaces Eifion in time. Reverend edits his own timeline. Eifion scrubs the exact hour he saw Catrin. Dylan changed what he said, 'it's happening again'. Everyone's trimming edges."

"Yes,' I said. "They're all engaged in narrative management."

"And someone is engaged in murder."

"Yes," I said.

He stopped pacing and looked at me properly.

"If it's not them," he said, "who?"

"It might be them," I said. "Or one of them. But that's not the immediate problem."

"What is?"

"We're still accepting too much as given," I said. "Especially in one area."

"Which?" he asked.

"The note," I said.

He glanced at the photograph of it pinned up.

"The 'truth makes cowards' one?"

"Yes," I said. "We've treated it as a threat addressed to Catrin. But it might not be."

"Come again?" he said.

I stepped closer to the photo.

"Look at the phrasing," I said. "We assumed the 'cowards' referred to people around her – villagers, perhaps – but the line is ambiguous. It could just as easily be the murderer trying to convince themselves that Catrin is the coward."

"You think it's self-justification," he said.

"Yes," I said. "Not intimidation. Those are different registers.

"And that changes what, exactly?" he asked.

"It changes who would write it," I said. "Threats outward and threats inward have different syntax. People who threaten others use direct address. People who threaten themselves hide behind aphorisms."

"Any suspects who like aphorisms?" he asked dryly.

"Yes," I said.

He waited. "Are you going to tell me?"

"Later," I said.

He swore under his breath. "You are absolutely infuriating."

"So I've been told," I said calmly.

The chapel door creaked open. Carys slipped inside, hair damp from the mist, her glasses fogged.

"Sorry," she said. "Mrs Pritchard has just informed half the village that I brought the 'death files' with me. I thought it best to remove myself."

'That's not quite what she said," Vaugh replied, "but close enough."

Carys managed a small, humourless smile. "How bad is it?"

"Worse than it looks," she said. "It always is."

"Eifion's dead," I said.

Her face changed – in two stages. First shock, then something narrower. Comprehension.

"Of course," she whispered.

"That's not the correct response," Vaugh said.

"It's no surprise, Inspector," she said quietly. "It's pattern recognition."

She stepped closer to the board, eyes moving quickly over the pinned notes.

"When we moved the 1992 records to central storage," she said. "We flagged three names as 'highly involved'. One of them was Eifion's father. One was Rhian's. One was Dylan's uncle."

"Yes," I said.

"And the others?" Vaugh asked.

"Parish representatives, company men, council officers," she said. "Some dead. Some retired. One left the country years ago. The rest stayed. People always think moving paper moves guilt."

Her voice was unexpectedly bitter.

It suited her.

'And you came here because Catrin had started unpicking that," I said.

"Yes," she said. "And because when people who unpick things suddenly die, the pattern tends to repeat."

"Which is a comforting thought," Vaugh muttered.

Carys glanced at him. "Comfort isn't my job, Inspector."

"No," I said. "It's mine."

They both looked at me.

"Not emotional comfort," I clarified. "Cognitive. I put things into an order that people can survive."

"And can they?" Carys asked.

"Not all of them," I said. "But more than if we leave the lies in charge."

She watched me for a moment, then nodded slightly, as if recognising a shared professional creed.

"Did you tell anyone you were coming here?" I asked her.

"Only my line manager," she said. "And she thought I was overreacting."

"And beside the anonymous email," I said. "Had there been any other…. Discouragement?"

Her jaw tightened.

She tapped her satchel.

"Last week," she said. "Someone left a copy of one of the old forms on my desk. No note. No context. Just the page with Reverend Lewis's signature and a red pen mark under it."

"Marked by whom?" Vaugh asked.

"No idea," she said. "The ink didn't match any of ours. But the message was obvious enough."

"Obvious how?" I asked.

"Look again," she said. "Or 'don't look further.' Hard to say which."

"The ambiguity may be deliberate," I said.

She rubbed her forehead. "I used to think records were neutral."

"They never are," I said.

Silence returned, not as weight but as density, pressing in at the edges.

Vaugh cleared his throat. "All right, so, where are we?"

"Multiple people are shaping their stories," I said. "But only one person is shaping events."

"And that person is…?" he prompted.

"Someone who believes they're protecting more than themselves," I said. "They think they are preserving the village."

"By killing its residents," he said.

"Yes," I said. "The logic is flawed but internally consistent."

He looked at the board again.

"What's our next move?" Carys asked.

"We re-interview Rhian," I said. "But not as a suspect."

"As what, then?" Vaugh asked.

"As what she is," I said. "A witness who has been carrying someone else's story for too long."

"And when she cracks?" he asked.

"She won't crack," I said. "She'll realign."

"Realign to what?" Carys asked.

"To truth," I said simply. "And when she does, the murderer will panic."

"And what's when we catch them?" Vaugh said.

"No," I said. "That's when they make their first visible mistake."

He gave me a look. "You don't think this second murder counts as a visible mistake?"

"No," I said. "Eifion's death looks like an accident to anyone who doesn't examine foot placement."

Carys eyed me. "You did."

"Yes," I said. "But the murderer did not plan for me."

"Who did they plan for?" she asked.

"Each other," I said. "They're not hiding from the police. They're hiding from the village."

A knock echoed from the chapel door.

Short.

Tentative.

Vaugh went to answer it.

Rhian stood there, hair damp, cardigan buttoned wrong, eyes fixed on something just past his shoulder.

"I..." she swallowed. "I think I remembered something. About that night. The... the first one."

She didn't say 1992.

She didn't have to.

Vaugh stepped back to let her in.

She crossed the threshold and shivered, not with cold, but with the awareness that she was entering a version of her life where the old stories would no longer fit.

Somewhere outside, unseen, the long coat moved again.

The village had begun telling the truth.

The murdered, knowingly or not, had reached the end of the map. There was no more room to shift the truth.

Chapter Sixteen – Rhian's Story

Rhian lingered in the threshold, cardigan buttoned askew, hair slipping from the clip she reserved for school mornings. She did not look frightened. She looked as if the ground itself had altered beneath her, leaving her adrift in a place she once understood.

Vaugh gestured to a chair. "Sit. Take your time."

She didn't sit.

She hovered, hands knotted at her waist, the posture of someone waiting for a verdict in a room that had never quite belonged to her.

"I don't want to make things worse," she said.

"But I can't… I can't keep holding it."

"Then don't," I said gently. "Just tell us what you remember."

Her throat moved in a swallow. "It's not a confession, she said quickly. "I haven't – I didn't."

"No one is assuming that," Vaugh said.

But Rhian looked at me, not him.

"You are," she whispered. "A little."

"I am assuming nothing," I said.

"Assumptions distort information. I want clarity, not confession."

She blinked rapidly, as if unused to that kind of reassurance.

"All right," she said shakily. "It's about the…the old event. The one everyone pretends didn't happen. The one with the plaque."

She gestured vaguely toward the chapel wall as if the plaque could hear her.

"I thought it was just an accident," she said.

"That's what Dad always said. He said there was nothing to be done, that sometimes things happen, and people have to learn to let them go."

"And did you?" I asked.

"I tried," she whispered. "We all did. But I saw something. Back then. And I think… I think Catrin found the same thing in the records."

Her hands trembled. She pressed her palms together, forcing the movement into stillness, as if she could contain the memory by sheer will.

"Go on," Vaugh said quietly.

"It was summer," she said. "School holidays. I was nine. There was a church picnic up by the old quarry. Everyone was there, all the families. They always did big picnics then."

She closed her eyes briefly, as if replaying the scene.

"The grown-ups were talking about the land inspection," she said. "The one before… before the accident. They were arguing, but quietly, like people do when children are around."

At last, she sat. The chair took her weight as if something inside her had given way, the scaffolding of memory shifting under its own strain.

"I wandered off," she said. "I was looking for a friend, I think. Or I was bored. I can't remember which. But I ended up behind the tool shed. You know the small one that's half-collapsed now."

"Yes," Vaugh said.

"I heard voices," she continued. "Men. My father was one of them. And Eifion's father. And...two others. Someone was angry. Really angry. They were saying someone needed to sign something properly. That it wasn't 'done right.' That it would cause trouble later'."

Her breathing quickened.

"It wasn't loud," she said. "It was the tone. Adults don't sound like that unless something is very wrong."

"What happened next?" I asked.

"I stepped on a branch," she said. "Just a small one. It cracked. The sound was nothing, really. But they all went quiet. Immediately."

Moisture gathered at the corners of her eyes, held there by a stubbornness that seemed older than she was.

"Dad called me over," she whispered. "He knelt and told me I hadn't heard anything important. That sometimes grown-ups get muddled when they're tired. He said he'd give me a lemon sherbet if I promised not to wander off again."

She shook her head.

"They were terrified," she said. "Not of me. Of what I might say."

"And what do you think they were talking about?" I asked.

"I don't know for certain," she said. "But after the accident… no one talked about it the same way again. And when the memorial went up – just the date, no names – dad said that it was for the best. That people heal faster when things aren't spelled out."

Her voice dropped to a whisper.

"But some people didn't heal. They carried it. And I think Catrin found something that meant they couldn't carry it quietly anymore."

I watched her. She did not lie. She circled the perimeter of a truth she had never been permitted to enter, tracing its outline in words she barely trusted.

"And you believe this is connected to Catrin's death?" Vaugh asked.

"Yes," she said immediately. "Because of what Eifion told me last week."

"What did he tell you?" I asked.

Her fingers twisted together.

"He said, 'Your father did what he thought was right. Don't hold that against him.'"

Vaugh and I exchanged a look.

"That could mean many things," Vaugh said cautiously.

"But he didn't stop there," she said. "He said, 'Catrin's stirring things. Things that were settled once. If people go pulling at threats, someone's going to get hurt again.'"

She wiped her eyes.

"I thought he meant gossip. I thought he meant arguments. I didn't think-'

She broke off.

I waited.

"When I saw him yesterday," she whispered, "he looked...resolved. Like he knew something was coming. And when he waved at me, it wasn't a casual wave. It was – "She swallowed. "It was a goodbye wave. I didn't realise it then, but I do now."

A long silence.

Vaugh leaned forward. "Rhian...why didn't you tell us this earlier?"

She let out a brittle laugh. "Because no one ever wants to hear the truth from me. I learnt that young. Dad said I 'misunderstood things.' Teachers said I was 'oversensitive'. People here don't like it when things get said too plainly."

"Plain is useful," I said.

She met my eyes. For the first time, something almost like trust flickered there.

"You're different," she whispered. "You look at things the way Catrin did."

"That is not always an advantage," I said.

She gave a small, choked laugh. Her mouth tightened, not in offence, but in recognition.

"No," she said. "I'm starting to see that."

She rubbed her sleeve across her eyes.

"There's one more thing," she said.

Vaugh stilled. "What thing?"

"A coat," she said. "A long dark one. I saw someone in it the night Catrin died."

My pulse altered, a subtle recalibration, as if my body had registered a change in atmospheric pressure.

"Where?" I asked.

"Up by the lane," she said. "Heading toward her cottage. I assumed it was the Reverend. He walks at night. But…but now I'm not sure."

"Why not?" Vaugh asked.

"Because the stride was wrong," she whispered. "It wasn't his. And it wasn't Eifion's. It was someone lighter. Quicker."

"And why didn't you mention it before?" I asked.

She looked down at her hands.

"Because whoever it was…they saw me."

A chill threaded itself through the chapel, quiet but insistent, as if the stones themselves had drawn breath.

"They slowed," she whispered. "Just for a moment. Like they were checking something, and then they walked on."

Vaugh leaned forward. "Rhian. Why are you telling us this now?"

She looked at me.

Because you're next.

It wasn't spoken this time.

But it hovered in the space between us.

"I'm telling you now," she said finally.

"Because when I saw Eifion's face this afternoon… I knew someone in this village was killing to keep something buried. And if they looked at me that night."

Her breath shuddered.

"Maybe they think I know something too."

I stood.

"Rhian," I said softly, "you are safe."

She laughed weakly. "No, I'm not. And neither are you."

Beyond the chapel walls, fog pressed against the glass, patient and expectant, as if it had come with its own intentions.

It was no longer the gentle veil of the morning.

It carried weight now, dense and deliberate.

It had gathered shape.

Someone moved within it, a shadow drawn in charcoal against the grey.

And time, which had once seemed generous, was narrowing to a point.

Chapter Seventeen – The Visitor at Dusk

The guest room above the Black Lion was small enough that if I stretched my arms out, my fingertips could have brushed opposite walls. I didn't test the theory; I prefer hypothetical measurements to unnecessary movement.

The wallpaper had once sported a pattern of climbing roses, now faded into a suggestion of itself. The single sash window looked down over the crossroads, where the butcher's shop, post office, chapel and lane formed a rough square. Bryngwyn's entire universe, compressed into four corners and a fog-prone centre.

Dusk had come early. The light outside had flattened into a blue-grey smear. The kind that makes it difficult to tell whether it is late afternoon or early evening without consulting a clock.

I had three.

My phone, the bedside alarm, and the watch on my wrist.

They all agreed. It was 17:42.

On the bed: my notebook, three photocopies, and a sheet torn from the hotel's complimentary pad. The slogan—Rest, Restore, Return—read as wishful thinking.

I drew a line down the centre of the sheet and began to list two words at the top of each column.

SPOKEN / RECORDED

Under *Spoken*, I wrote:

- Rhian: saw Eifion 'about half four'

- Reverend: 'indoors all evening, quiet night'

- Dylan: 'saw Catrin once, basket, head down'

- Eifion: 'saw her heading down the lane' (no time)

Under *Recorded*, I wrote:

- School register: Rhian with the after-school club until 16:45

- Jenkin's log: Reverend 'walked, but not as far as usual'

- Delivery sheet: meat delivery signed by Dylan at 16:15

- Train arrival: my own at 10:32; constable's patrol log matched

The discrepancy was minor. Almost trivial. But that was where the most dangerous lies began: in the gap between two things that should align and do not.

I circled the school register entry.

Rhian had shifted herself by approximately fifteen minutes.

The Reverend had shifted himself by several hours.

Eifion had shifted himself out of precision altogether.

None of that yet proved murder.

But it proved something important: Bryngwyn was reconstructing itself around absence.

There was a soft thump from below. A door closing, voices rising briefly as the evening crowd arrived at the bar. A faint scent of frying oil drifted up through the floorboards, carrying with it the ghost of other diners' meals.

A knock came at my door. Three short raps evenly spaced.

"Come in," I said.

PC Ellis opened the door cautiously, as though unsure whether I might bite.

"Evening, DS Pryce," he said. "Mrs Griffiths sent up a tray. She says you've eaten nothing today but 'interference and homicide' and that neither counts as proper food."

He carried a tray bearing a bowl of soup, two slices of bread, and a mug of tea that proclaimed, 'Best Nan in Ceredigion'. I chose not to ask.

"Thank you," I said.

He set the tray down on the small bedside table, eyeing the spread of papers.

"Looks...organised," he said.

"It isn't yet," I replied. "That's the problem."

He shuffled, then nodded towards the window. "Place feels different tonight."

"How so?" I asked.

He glanced outside, though the fog showed nothing of use.

"Quieter," he said. "Only not really. More like people are making noises to hide the quiet. Doors are being shut more loudly than usual. Coughing outside when no one's ill. That sort of thing."

"A performance of normality," I said.

"Yes," he said, as if grateful for a phrase. "Exactly."

He hesitated.

"Sergeant Jenkins wanted me to tell you there are increased patrols by the cottages," he added. "Just in case."

"In case what?" I asked.

"In case whoever did this decides they haven't done enough," he said.

A practised concern.

"Do you feel safe?" he asked, somewhat abruptly.

It was not a question officers usually asked consultants.

"I feel observed," I said. "Safety is a separate parameter."

He grimaced. "If you need anything. Extra patrols, life to the stations, whatever. Call me. I'm on until midnight."

"I will," I said. "Thank you."

He hesitated again, hand on the doorframe.

"Do you think it's someone I know?" he asked quietly. "Someone I say hello to in the shop?"

"Yes," I said.

He flinched. "You don't soften things, do you?"

"No," I said. "But I don't exaggerate either. That's something."

He gave a short, uncertain laugh.

"Right," he said. "Well. Enjoy the soup. Try to sleep"

"Sleep is aspirational," I said.

He left, shaking his head.

I ate half the soup, more out of obligation than appetite. My mind insisted on returning to Rhian's account of the long coat, the Reverend's half-admission, Eifion's unfinished sentence in his notebook.

IF THEY FIND OUT I KNEW, THEY'LL THINK I –

Think I what?

Participated?

Benefited?

Failed to act?

Or think I killed?

The thought lodged unpleasantly.

I folded the hotel pad sheet and slid it into my notebook. The room had grown darker. I switched on the small bedside lamp. The bulb hummed faintly, a high, constant sound I suspected more people would ignore.

I couldn't.

To distract myself, I opened the evidence photo of the note left with Catrin and enlarged the handwriting on my phone.

Truth makes cowards of the unprepared.

I traced the letters with my gaze. The 'ts' were crossed slightly high, the 'rs' open, the 'ds' closed tight. The loops on the 'hs' weren't loops at all, just straight vertical lines with a hook.

I had seen those hooks elsewhere, but my brain refused to present the location on command. It would surface later, as it always did, like a photograph developing in slow solution.

Another knock sounded.

Softer this time.

Two taps, not three.

"Come in," I said.

No one entered.

I stood, crossed the room, and opened the door.

The corridor was empty. The light at the far end flickered once, then steadied.

Somewhere downstairs, someone laughed too loudly at something that wasn't that funny.

At my feet, on the worn carpet, lay an envelope.

No name.

No address.

Just a plain white envelope, sealed.

I picked it up and closed the door carefully.

The paper was cheap, and the seal was misaligned. Whoever assembled this was not used to stationery as a display. That, in itself, was notable.

I opened it with a fingernail, careful not to tear the interior.

There was one sheet inside.

A single line, printed in heavy blue ballpoint.

YOU DON'T BELONG HERE

No signature.

No extra flourish.

I re-read it twice.

"You," underscored once, the line biting into the paper.'

Don't.

Not *shouldn't.*

Not *mustn't.*

Don't.

Belong here.

A statement. Not a threat.

Implied threat, yes – but structurally, it was a classification.

I sat back down on the bed and placed the new note beside the photograph of the earlier one.

Truth makes cowards of the unprepared.

You don't belong here.

Different handwriting.

Different emotional register.

"Three authors," I said aloud.

The first: Catrin's killer, seeking justification in aphorism.

The second: the anonymous emailer to Carys, all jagged fear and no grammar.

The third: this.

Someone who could have said, *Go home* or *Leave*, but instead chose *You don't belong*.

Belonging was a social concept. People who chose that language were less concerned with personal danger, more with maintaining a structure. A system.

Someone invested in Bryngwyn's cohesion.

Reverend?

Possibly.

Mrs Pritchard?

Also, possibly.

Dylan?

Unlikely. His speech was harsher. He preferred concrete nouns rather than abstractions.

Rhian?

No. Her writing. The labels in her classroom, I had noticed earlier. Curved in a different direction, loops more generous, spacing more hesitant.

I examined the Y.

The tail hooked slightly to the left before descending. Then it struck me. The hymn list pinned on the chapel's noticeboard had the same hooked capitals.

Not Reverend Thomas's next script, which adorned the sermon notes.

Someone else's writing.

Someone who liked being useful enough to take on practical tasks, and invisible enough that no one commented on it.

My brain sifted through images.

Not Rhian.

Not Carys.

The vestry door.

The chapel kitchen.

The list of rota names.

I set the thought aside. Forced retrieval would only blur it.

Outside, the last light thinned. The lane below blurred into a band of shadow and damp.

I stood and moved to the window.

From here, I could see the crossroads clearly: the glow from the butcher's shop, thin light seeping from the post office, the darker outline of the chapel. Beyond it, the lane curved toward

Catrin's cottage and, further still, up to where the old footpath sign leaned into the hedge.

A figure stood by the sign.

Tall.

Long coat.

Still.

Too still.

People at rest fidget.

This figure did not.

The figure shifted, as if aware of being watched, turning its head toward the inn. I stepped back from the window, pressing against the wall. My heart rate climbed—measured, but not deniable.

I counted silently.

Twenty-two seconds.

Then I edged back to the glass, keeping to one side.

The figure was gone.

Fog drifted around the sign, innocent once more.

I returned to the bed and wrote one line in my notebook:

COAT WATCHES CHAPEL AND INN.

Below it, another:

THREAT NOTE ≠ KILLER NOTE. DIFFERENT HAND. DIFFERENT FEAR.

My phone vibrated—a text from Vaugh.

Vaugh: Rhian, home. Carys is back at B&B. Patrols set. You alright?

Me: Received an anonymous note. No immediate aggression. Implied exclusion.

There was a longer pause than usual before his reply.

Vaugh: That counts as aggression here.

Me: I'm not leaving.

Vaugh: I didn't think you would. Lock your door.

I locked the door.

Not because I thought it would keep danger out, but because it would make noise if someone tried the door. Noise was data.

I lay back on the bed fully clothed, notebook open on my chest, pen in hand.

Every so often, a car passed on the main road beyond the village, its sound dampened by distance and fog. Downstairs, laughter rose and fell like an unreliable tide. Somewhere further off, a dog barked once, then twice.

I waited for the quiet that meant something was about to happen.

It didn't come.

Instead, my mind supplied an entirely unhelpful image: Rhian as a child, behind the shed, hearing adults argue about signatures and 'doing what's right', then being bought off with lemon sherbets.

Bryngwyn had never taught its children to tell the truth. Only to carry other peoples.

Now one of those children had grown up and begun to speak.

And someone in a long, dark coat was standing in the fog, deciding what to do about it.

The visitor at dusk had not come to see me.

Not yet.

They were measuring something.

The village's tolerance, perhaps.

Or their own.

Chapter Eighteen — Pressure Points

Morning arrived without ceremony. A pale wash of colour pressed thinly across Bryngwyn's sky. The fog had retreated to its usual crouch in the fields, leaving the village exposed in a clarity that felt intrusive, as if the light had revealed something meant to stay hidden.

I descended the stairs of the Black Lion with my notebook in hand. The bar was empty except for Mrs Griffiths, who was polishing glasses with the brisk energy of someone for whom hard work was the only known antidote to worry.

"You didn't sleep," she said by way of greeting.

'No," I replied. "There were noises."

"There is always noise," she said. "The trick is not hearing them."

"I don't possess that trick," I said.

She huffed, half-sympathy, half-exasperation.

"Inspector Vaugh is waiting outside," she added. "He said to tell you that he's had it up to here with villagers who think they can simultaneously demand answers and withhold half the truth.”

“That seems accurate,” I said.

I thanked her, stepped out, and found Vaugh leaning against the patrol car, arms folded, jaw set.

“You got my text?” he asked.

“Yes,” I said. “A new statement?”

“No. Worse. Three.”

“From?” I asked.

“Mrs Morgan. Now, suddenly convinced, she saw a figure ‘lurking’ near the post office three nights ago. Though she can’t describe them. Dylan, claiming he thinks someone’s been watching the butcher’s yard. And Mrs Hafod from the chapel choir, saying she heard footsteps behind her last night but decided she ‘didn’t want to make a fuss’.”

“That is not helpful,” I said.

“No,” he agreed. “But welcome to the part of a murder inquiry where everyone realises their imagination has legs.”

He pulled open the passenger door for me—a chivalrous gesture, though likely born of habit rather than intent.

"We need to triage these," he said.

"We also need to interview the Reverend again," I said. "Preferably before he constructs a more palatable version or last night."

"Agreed," he said. "And Rhian."

"She should rest," I said. "But she won't."

"No," he murmured. "She won't."

We drove toward the chapel first. It was the new centre of gravity. The place everyone watched without admitting it.

Carys waited inside, papers spread across the altar table like a very secular offering. She had organised the records into neat stacks, each labelled with yellow tabs.

"Morning," she said without looking up. "I found something."

"That's becoming a worrying refrain," Vaugh said.

She slid a sheet toward me.

It was a copy of the old parish rota from 1992.

Fundraisers, Cleaning duties. Hymn selection volunteers.

A list of names.

Twenty-three of them.

Some familiar.

Some not.

My gaze went immediately to the handwriting.

The capital letters.

The hooked Y.

The slightly crooked descending lines.

I felt the pieces align, not with drama, but with quiet inevitability.

"The note," I said.

Carys blinked. "What note?"

I held up the envelope delivered last night. "This. The handwriting matches this rota list."

She leaned in, eyebrows raised. "Are you certain?"

"Yes," I said. "Stroke direction, pressure points, slant angle. Identical."

Vaugh crossed his arms. "So, someone who helped run the chapel left you a warning."

"Yes," I said. "Someone who believes in the structure more than the message."

"Which name?" Carys asked.

"The one who writes the rota," I said. "Not the Reverend. The Reverend doesn't have that handwriting. He prints when annotating margins but uses cursive elsewhere. This person uses a hybrid."

Carys tapped a finger along the list. "Most of these people are gone," she said.

Then, after a moment: "Or dead."

I pointed halfway down the sheet.

G. Pritchard.

Organist.

Rota Coordinator.

Flower committee.

And, in small, neat script, "Steward duties."

Vaugh stared at the name. "Mrs Pritchard?"

"Yes," I said.

"She left you the note?" he asked.

"It's probable," I said. "She wanted me to feel unwelcome, not endangered. The structure of the message is exclusionary, not violent."

"She's protective," Carys murmured. "Of the Chape. Of the village."

"And of the story they built after the accident," I said.

Vaugh's jaw tightened. "And would she kill for it?"

"No," I said. "But she would warn for it."

"Then who?" he began.

"-Would kill for it?" I finished. "Someone who believed preserving that story is more essential than preserving a life."

"Which is becoming a pattern," Carys added grimly.

Vaugh paced once, then twice, rubbing his hand along the back of his neck.

"All right," he said. "Let's assume Mrs Pritchard is the village's warning system, not the murderer. That still leaves us with someone who killed Eifion in broad daylight."

"And left no evidence," Carys said quietly.

"Incorrect," I said.

They both turned to me.

"What evidence?" Vaugh asked.

"The absence," I said.

Vaugh groaned. "Always the absence."

"It's valuable," I said. "If someone leaves nothing behind physically, they leave something behind behaviourally."

Carys frowned. "Which behaviour this time?"

"Their choice of victim," I said.

I stepped closer to the board and tapped Eifion's photograph.

"Eifion was the most likely to talk," I said. "But also, the one most likely to be believed about what he saw."

"How does that help us?"

"He was chosen," I said simply. "Not because he knew the most, but because he would admit the most.

Carys stared at me. "You think the killer is someone who knows which villagers are likely to protect others versus protect themselves."

"Yes," I said.

"That's half the village," Vaugh muttered.

"No," I said. "Only the ones who have been watching people closely for years."

Something flickered at the edge of my thoughts. Something about the handwriting. Not the shapes, those I had already identified, but the spacing.

The spacing

On the rota sheet, the letters huddled together as if trying to stay warm. On the note, the words were spaced exactly the same way: tight at the start of the line, drifting wider toward the end.

A person who wrote in a hurry.

Not panicked hurry.

Rehearsed hurry.

Someone accustomed to writing while standing.

Or while doing something else.

I pictured the chapel.

Who wrote standing?

Who always stood?

The organist.

Mrs Pritchard, yes, but also –

The thought clicked.

"Where's the Reverend?" I asked.

"Home, I assume," Vaugh said.

"No," I said. "He walks every morning. To the edge of the lane, then turns back."

"Routine," Carys said.

"Yes," I replied. "And if his routine has shifted in the last twenty-four hours, that matters."

"Why?" Vaugh asked.

"Because people under pressure change their routes," I said. "And their patterns. And their stories."

Vaugh let out a slow breath. "All right. We'll talk to him. Again."

I nodded, though my attention had drifted back to the handwriting.

It wasn't the Reverend's.

But it was someone close to him.

Someone who shared tasks with him.

Someone Rhian had described earlier:

"Trying not to make a fuss."

"Always helping."

Another detail surfaced.

The memorial plaque.

I had seen a small slip of paper tucked behind it two days ago—a garden rota.

With the same handwriting.

I slid my notebook across the table and wrote one new line:

HANDWRITING ≠ THREAT AUTHOR ≠ KILLER. BUT A WARNING COMES FROM NEAR THE CHAPEL. OBSERVE VOLUNTEERS.

Carys watched me write. "You're narrowing it."

"Yes," I said. "But not the way you think."

Vaugh grabbed his coat. "Let's go speak to the Reverend before the whole village starts rewriting its day."

We stepped out into the lane. A thin wind traced its fingers through the hedgerow.

Somewhere down the hill, a dog barked once. High and anxious.

As we approached the vicarage, I caught sight of a figure near the side path.

Long coat.

Still.

Watching.

But when I blinked, the path was empty.

Not vanished.

Relocated.

Someone was measuring us again.

"Pryce," Vaugh said. "You alright?"

"Yes," I said.

I wasn't certain the village could say the same.

Chapter Nineteen – The Reverend's Distance

The vicarage stood slightly apart from the other cottages, not by design but by habit.

The hedges had been shaped with a kind of resigned precision, more a matter of routine than aesthetics. Windows without streaks, path without debris, door painted a blue that gestured at hospitality but withheld commitment.

Reverend Thomas Lewis answered our knock almost immediately.

He wore the uniform of rural movement: shoes built for mud, a jacket that remembered rain, scarf arranged with habitual neatness. His hair had faded to a soft grey, a misleading signal of gentleness. The smile he offered was a technicality, confined to the mouth, the eyes remaining elsewhere.

"Inspector," he said. "And Miss Pryce. I wondered when you'd come."

"That's not usually how people greet the police," Vaugh said.

"No," the Reverend agreed mildly. "But I've buried enough villagers to know when the rhythm changes."

He stepped aside to let us in.

The sitting room held a measured warmth. Beeswax and the dry, fibrous scent of old paper lingered at the edges.

Order prevailed. Sermon notes aligned in a stack, spectacles folded with intent and balanced on a Bible, a notebook opened but untouched on the chair's arm.

The notebook's pages were untouched. I registered this at once.

"Please," he said. "Sit."

We did not.

"I understand Eifion has died," he said, before Vaugh could speak. "A tragic accident."

"An accident?" Vaugh echoed.

The Reverend inclined his head. "So, I'm told."

"Who told you?" I asked.

He hesitated—a fraction of a second too long.

"Mrs Pritchard," he said. "She rang this morning."

I logged that for later.

"And before that?" Vaugh asked. "Before you heard anything official?"

The Reverend folded his hands. "I suppose I sensed something was wrong. People do come to me with worries, Inspector."

"Last night?" Vaugh pressed.

"Yes," the Reverend said smoothly. "Last night as well."

"Who?" Vaugh asked.

The Reverend's gaze drifted, just enough to register, in the direction of the window.

"Several parishioners," he said. "They were unsettled after Catrin's death. And then Eifion's...fall."

"You're skipping ahead," Vaugh said. "Last night Eifion was alive."

The Reverend smiled faintly. "So, we all were."

"That wasn't the question," Vaugh said.

Silence arrived and the Reverend handled it with the ease of someone who has practiced its application.

"Reverend Lewis," I said. "You told Sergeant Jenkins that you went for a walk last night."

"Yes," he said. "I find walking helps me think."

"You told us earlier you stayed in," Vaugh said.

"I said I stayed in *mostly*," he replied gently. "Perhaps my phrasing was unclear."

"It was," I said. "And unnecessarily so."

His eyes found me, the focus sharpening.

"Miss Pryce," he said. "You must understand that in a village like this, words are chosen carefully."

"Yes," I said. "And sometimes rearranged."

A line appeared where his mouth had been.

"I walked to the end of the lane," he said. "No further."

"At what time?" Vaugh asked.

"After evening prayers," he said. "Around eight."

"Eight o'clock," Vaugh repeated. "That's quite precise."

"I had just finished writing my sermon," he said. "I glanced at the clock."

"Which sermon?" I asked.

He gestured to the Bible. "This Sundays."

"May I see your notes?" I asked.

His brows rose slightly. "I'm not accustomed to…"

"I'm not interested in theology," I said. "Only sequence."

A pause measured and deliberate.

Then he handed me the notebook.

Every page was blank.

"You haven't written anything yet," Vaugh said.

"No," the Reverend said calmly, "I prefer to compost mentally."

"That's unusual," Vaugh said.

"It's efficient," the Reverend replied.

"It's risky," I said. "Memory is malleable."

His attention fixed on me, intent and unblinking.

"You think I'm lying," he said.

"I think you're curating," I replied. "There's a difference."

"And what would I be curating?" he asked.

"A version of events in which you are peripheral," I said.

Vaugh stepped in. "Reverend, did you see Eifion last night?"

The Reverend hesitated again, the interval longer now.

"Yes," he said.

"When?" Vaugh asked.

"Briefly," he said. "I passed his gate. We exchanged words."

"What words?" Vaugh asked.

"He asked me whether I thought some truths were better left...dormant."

"And what did you say?" Vaugh pressed.

The Reverend folded his hands again. "I said that truth without compassion can harm."

"Did you threaten him?" Vaugh asked.

"No," he said sharply. "Of course not."

"Did you warn him?" I asked.

His jaw tightened.

"I reminded him of our responsibility to the living," he said. "Not the dead."

"And how did he respond?" I asked.

"He said the dead were already living with them," the Reverend said quietly. "Whether we acknowledge them or not."

The room contracted, air thickening by degrees.

"Reverend," Vaugh said, "where were you when Eifion fell?"

"I was at home," he said. "Preparing for bed."

"At what time?" Vaugh asked.

"Just after nine."

"That conflicts with the neighbour who heard voices near Eifion's at half past nine," Vaugh said.

The Reverend looked genuinely surprised.

"Does it?"

"Yes," Vaugh said. "And with the dogs barking."

"The dogs bark at everyone," the Reverend said.

"Not like that," I said. "They barked recognition, not alarm."

I caught a brief disturbance—irritation, quickly suppressed.

"You're very certain," he said.

"Yes," I replied. "Because animals do not lie to preserve social cohesion."

His gaze shifted elsewhere.

"I did not kill Eifion," he said quietly. "Nor Catrin. I have devoted my life to care."

"I believe that" I said.

He turned back to me sharply.

"You do?"

"Yes," I said. "Which is why I don't think you are the person we are looking for."

Vaugh shot me a look.

"But" I continued. "I do think you are protecting someone."

The Reverend's composure cracked. Not completely. But enough.

"I am protecting my daughter," he said.

Silence arrived, brittle and sudden.

"From what?" Vaugh asked carefully.

"From inheriting our sins," he said. "From being dragged into a past she had no power to change."

"Did Rhian know about the signatures?" Vaugh asked.

The Reverend closed his eyes.

"She knew fragments," he said. "Too much for a child. Too little to act on."

"And when Catrin began asking questions?" I asked.

"I told Rhian to stay away from it," he said. "I told her some things were not hers to carry."

"And did she?" Vaugh asked.

"I don't know," he admitted.

That, finally, registered as honest.

"Reverend," Vaugh said, "someone left a note for Miss Pryce last night. A warning."

The Reverend looked startled. "What kind of warning?"

"About belonging," I said.

He exhaled slowly. "That sounds like Mrs Pritchard."

"Yes," I said. "It does."

"She means well," he said quickly.

"I know," I said. "Which is why she is not the murderer."

The Reverend's shoulders sagged slightly, relief leaking through despite his efforts.

"Then who?" he asked quietly.

I studied him for a long moment.

"Someone who learned early that silence is rewarded," I said. "Someone who believes control is kindness. Someone who thinks they are preventing harm."

His eyes widened, not with fear, but with the recognition of a pattern.

"Rhian wouldn't." he began.

"I didn't say she would," I said. "I said she might think she has to."

Vaugh's head snapped toward me.

"You think....?"

"I think," I said carefully, "that Rhian is not our murderer."

Relief registered, brief and involuntary.

"But" I continued, "I think the murderer is someone who believes they are acting for her."

The Reverend swallowed.

"Who??" Vaugh asked.

The Reverend didn't answer.

He didn't need to.

The outline of the lie resolved itself at last.

And it did not belong to the person everyone had been watching.

Chapter Twenty-One — Carys Morgan

Carys Morgan had not always been called that.

Once, she had been Anwen Rhydderch, and she had never intended to come back.

As Anwen, she had grown up in Bryngwyn when the quarry still thrummed with the illusion of permanence. Her childhood soundscape was lorries on the lane and men's voices carrying from the hillside, chapel on Sundays, school on weekdays, the same faces at every threshold.

She had been the sort of girl adults described as "sensible". She remembered things. She knew which families were on good terms and which had whispers of arguments. She fetched forgotten parcels from the post office and messages from the chapel porch, moving through the village as if it were a series of rooms in a single, familiar house.

She also knew when conversations stopped as she approached.

When the quarry accident happened, Anwen was old enough to understand it and young enough to be blamed for understanding too much. She had been there that day, delivering sandwiches, the way she often did. She had seen men argue in a way they later insisted they had not. She had seen a clipboard change hands, a piece of paper folded too quickly, a signature obtained with too much insistence.

Later, when the shock had spent itself, when grief had settled into something flatter and more dangerous, Anwen began to ask questions.

Not aggressively.
Not loudly.

Just... precisely.

Why had the inspection been rushed?
Why had certain reports been filed and others not?
Why did the plaque carry only a date and no names?

Initially, there were compliments about her 'good brain.' Then came warnings about 'dwelling.' Eventually, silence. Doors closed with increased efficiency. Eye contact became a rarity.

One evening, her father had said, in a voice that did not invite comment:

"You're making things worse."

She had not understood how that could be true. The accident had already happened. It could not be unhappened by silence.

Bryngwyn had little use for causality. Its focus was the mechanics of survival.

Anwen applied to a college in the city. No one stopped her. Some seemed relieved. She left with one suitcase, a grant, and the vague sense that she was doing the village a kindness by removing the problem of her observation.

In the city, she discovered two things.

First, that anonymity felt like freedom. No one there had expectations of her, beyond the work she did. She became efficient, precise, and valuable. She learned how to speak softly and neutrally, how to ask questions that did not sound like accusations. She discovered she could become invisible when she wished.

Second, that forgetting was not the same as leaving something behind. Bryngwyn lived in the back of her mind like a room she had closed the door on but never locked. Every news report about industrial oversight tugged at it. Every case study on workplace accidents made the door rattle.

When she came back, nearly a decade later, she did not come back as Anwen Rhydderch.

She arrived instead as Carys Morgan.

It was not a complicated reinvention. She did not forge documents or falsify records. She simply... rearranged herself.

She used her middle name, Carys, which had always sat quietly in official forms. Morgan was her maternal grandmother's surname, honest enough to withstand scrutiny. Her hair was cut differently. Her clothes were plainer. Her speech had acquired the careful smoothness of someone who had learned not to alarm people.

When she presented herself to the chapel as "Carys Morgan, back to Wales after years in the city", no one questioned it too closely. People in Bryngwyn remembered what it cost to look things directly in the eye. A woman who offered competence and discretion was welcome, whatever she called herself.

Some recognised her, of course.

No one passes a childhood in Bryngwyn without leaving residue. Those who recognised her also remembered the accident, the elevation and suppression of voices, the plaque that recorded only a date.

They had no appetite for resurrecting ghosts.

If Carys Morgan wished to be Carys Morgan, they were willing to let Anwen Rhydderch drift quietly into the category of "people we once knew" without specifying further.

Carys took on tasks.

She cleaned the chapel. She sorted the records. She mended hymn books and suggested rota systems during meetings when everyone else had run out of patience. She remembered anniversaries without being asked. She developed the habit of standing at the back of any gathering, hands loosely folded, prepared to be useful.

In time, people referred to her as if she had always been present. Not accurate, not entirely false. More convenient: a narrative that met the teller's requirements.

When the memorial plaque was proposed, Carys argued, gently, for brevity.

"A date," she said, "so we remember. But names… names can reignite things best left quiet. The families will have their own places to grieve."

It was not a lie.

It simply omitted the part where Anwen, years before, had stood at the edge of a preparatory meeting and watched men decide which words would appear in public and which would not.

When Catrin Hughes began quietly requesting old records, Carys noticed at once.

Catrin had the same dangerous quality Anwen had possessed: curiosity without an off switch. She read minutes, traced signatures, and asked what had happened to certain files gone "missing". She used words like 'accountability' and 'history'.

She reminded Carys of a person Carys had chosen not to be.

Carys warned her, at first.

"Be careful with what you find," she said in the chapel kitchen, in a tone that could be taken as general advice. "Some things here are held together by not being said."

When warning failed, Carys reassured herself.

Catrin was clever, certainly, but a single notebook was insufficient to dismantle three decades of curated omission.

Then Eifion Davies began looking nervous when Catrin's name was mentioned.

Carys recognised the signs.

He had been Anwen's friend, once. He remembered the sharpness of her questions. He remembered the way her persistence had unsettled grown men. If he had been carrying something since then, Carys understood the weight.

She also understood what would happen to Bryngwyn if he dropped it.

By the time Serene Pryce arrived, Carys had been performing stability for so long that she had mistaken the performance for reality. The village leaned on her. The Reverend relied on her. Mrs Pritchard assumed she would fill any gap that appeared in a rota. Rhian used her as an emotional anchor when her father turned inwards.

Carys had become the hinge on which the village swung.

The difficulty with being a hinge: eventually, one mistakes oneself for the door.

When Catrin died, Carys's first thought was not *What have I done?*

It was a calculation:

What must be supported, to maintain structural integrity?

When Eifion fell, the question became:

If I let go, who will carry this?

And when Serene, with her forensic attention and unwillingness to be soothed by incomplete answers, walked out of the mist and into Bryngwyn, Carys recognised at once what she was.

Not an outsider.
Not a threat in the sense that the village would name.

She functioned as a mirror.

Not for Bryngwyn.
For Anwen.

For a girl who had once asked the wrong questions and had left because no one wanted to hear the answers.

Carys had invested years constructing a life with no space for Anwen.

Serene's presence suggested that this effort had been temporary.

The note Carys left for Serene — *You don't belong here* — was not written in rage.

It was composed in fear.

Not that Serene would destroy the village.

That Serene would unlock a version of Carys that had been buried so effectively that Carys herself had begun to forget her.

For a while, she told herself that she was killing for the village.

That she killed for duty, for protection, for continuity.

It was only later, sitting at her own kitchen table with two detectives watching her, that she realised something worse:

She had also killed for Anwen.

To punish anyone who tried to do in 2020 what Anwen had been too young and too isolated to complete in 1992.

By the time she understood this, the distinction no longer mattered to the dead.

Chapter Twenty-two – The One No One Watched

Vaugh parked the patrol car farther from Carys Morgan's cottage than was strictly necessary.

"Last chance to tell me I'm wrong," he said.

"You're not wrong," I replied.

He exhaled through his nose, a sound that mapped closely to annoyance but stopped short.

"Just once," he said, "I'd like to be."

The lane registered as quiet. A dog barked, the sound habitual rather than reactive. The air was thin, washed out, the light receding as if clocking off for the day.

Carys's cottage looked as it always did. Hedge neat, step swept, curtains open just enough to suggest welcome without inviting investigation. The front door was on the latch.

Inside, the radio supplied the residue of a farming programme. The hallway held the layered scents of polish and potatoes.

Carys stood in the kitchen, sleeves rolled, drying a mug.

She turned when she heard us enter and smiled. Not a wide smile. A polite, measured one.

"Inspector. Serene," she said. "I thought you might come."

"That's not usually the first reaction to the police," Vaugh said.

"I've seen a great many reactions," Carys replied. "Panic is rarely useful."

She set the mug down and folded the towel with careful movements. Keys hung beside the back door: chapel, vestry, hall, assorted unlabelled ones that had become hers by default when others forgot or moved or died.

"Sit, if you like," she said.

We did not sit.

"Carys," Vaugh began, "we have some questions."

"Yes," she said. "I imagine you do."

"You've lived in Bryngwyn for—" he began.

"Twenty-two years," she supplied.

"You told us you came out from the city," he said.

"I said I'd been in the city before I came back to Wales," she replied. "People assumed the rest."

"You didn't correct them," I said.

She shrugged, a minimal concession. 'It seemed... the more merciful option.'

"To whom?" I asked.

Carys tilted her head, considering the question properly.

"To everyone," she said. "Including myself."

Vaugh reached into his folder and took out a photocopy. He laid it on the table.

It was a school photograph, faded at the edges. Children stood squinting in weak sunshine, some neat, some dishevelled, all arranged in rows that pretended order.

Near the centre, a girl of about fourteen.

Dark hair pulled back. Eyes direct. Chin set with familiar determination.

Carys looked at it.

For a measurable interval, her expression remained static.

Then her shoulders shifted, almost imperceptibly, a slackening that suggested the release of a long-held breath.

"Where did you get that?" she asked quietly.

"Old school register," Vaugh said. "The Reverend helped us. He remembered there was a photograph."

"Anwen Rhydderch," I said, tapping the name beneath the image. "Bryngwyn Comprehensive."

Carys's gaze moved from the photograph to me.

"Do you think this is a revelation to me?" she asked. "I was there when it was taken."

"People here think Carys Morgan came from away," Vaugh said. "From some city, some other life."

"They didn't want Anwen back," Carys said. "They wanted competence. I obliged."

"And you let them pretend you were new," I said.

"I let them pretend a great many things," she said. "It was how we all survived."

"Until Catrin stopped pretending," I said.

Silence. Not absence, but density.

"Why don't you tell us what happened, Anwen?" Vaugh said.

She flinched at the name, just once.

"Don't," she said softly. "That girl is gone."

"She never left," I said. "She just changed her label."

Carys's eyes met mine. For the first time since I had arrived in Bryngwyn, something unguarded showed there.

"You're very certain of yourself," she said.

"No," I replied. "I'm very certain of the pattern."

She gave a small, humourless laugh.

"I suppose that's what they pay you for," she said.

"They pay me to notice where stories don't quite match," I replied.

Vaugh leaned against the counter.

"Carys Morgan, also known as Anwen Rhydderch," he said carefully, "were you at Catrin Hughes' cottage the night she died?"

"Yes," she said.

"Did you follow her from the henhouse?" he asked.

"Yes."

"Did you break her door?" he continued.

"Yes."

"Did you push her?" he asked.

Carys closed her eyes.

"Yes," she said.

The radio continued, undisturbed. An advertisement for animal feed filled the gap, its timing misaligned with the room.

"Why?" Vaugh asked.

She opened her eyes again.

"Because I've already watched this village tear itself apart once," she said. "I wasn't going to watch it do it again for the sake of someone's idea of truth."

"That someone being Catrin," I said.

"She was clever," Carys said. "Like Anwen. Clever people are very dangerous when they arrive at the wrong time."

"Is there a right time?" I asked.

Carys's mouth twisted.

"Apparently not," she said.

"And Eifion Davies?" Vaugh asked. "Did you go to his house?"

"Yes."

"Did you push him?" he asked.

"Yes," she said. "Not hard. I didn't think—"

"You didn't think it would kill him," I finished. "You didn't think gravity applies more strictly to a guilty conscience."

A tiny spark of anger lit in her eyes.

"He was never guilty of anything but weakness," she snapped. "He signed what he was told to sign. He kept quiet when he was told to. Same as everyone else."

"And you?" I asked.

"I tried to keep them intact," she said. "Someone had to."

"You keep saying that", I said. "'Someone had to'."

Carys's jaw clenched.

"Because it's true," she said.

"No," I said. "Because it's what you decided made it acceptable to choose who lived with which knowledge and who didn't live at all."

We regarded one another across the narrow kitchen.

"You think I enjoyed any of this?" she asked quietly.

"No," I said. "That's what makes it terrifying."

Vaugh straightened.

"Carys Morgan, born Anwen Rhydderch," he said, voice formal now, "I am arresting you on suspicion of the murders of Catrin Hughes and Eifion Davies."

Carys didn't resist when he moved behind her and cuffed her wrists. She watched me as he did it, neither accusing nor pleading.

"I left once to stop being the girl who upset people," she said. "I came back to be the woman who kept them steady."

"And you killed to keep them steady," I said.

"Yes," she replied simply.

"Do you think they'll forgive you?" I asked.

She directed her gaze to the window, the hedge outside occluding most of the landscape.

"They'll say they hate me," she said. "Some of them will mean it. Some of them won't. Most of them will be grateful they don't have to look at themselves too closely."

"Is that what you want?" I asked.

She processed the question.

"I wanted to be necessary," she said. "Unfortunately, I succeeded."

Vaugh guided her toward the door.

She paused at the threshold, a final interval.

"Do you think you'd have done differently?" she asked me. "If you'd been the one left here when everyone else broke?"

"Yes," I said.

She studied my face, calibrating for certainty.

"I hope you're right," she said. "For everyone's sake."

Then she stepped out into the lane, no longer unseen.

Chapter Twenty-three — What Remains

Bryngwyn did not gather to watch Carys Morgan leave.

That was the village's final act of control: to remove her quietly, as though removal could be mistaken for resolution.

No figures at the windows. No clusters at the lane corners. Doors latched. Curtains half-drawn, calibrated to admit only as much light as could be tolerated. The village seemed unable to look directly at what it had allowed.

The police car departed without ceremony.

Routine reasserted itself with the efficiency of habit. Bryngwyn resumed its pattern, as if nothing had been interrupted.

By midday, the butcher's sign was flipped to OPEN. Dylan's sleeves were rolled, his jaw set, each cut of meat measured and deliberate, hands occupied, as if idle hands might betray him. At the post office, Mrs Morgan stood behind

Mrs Hafod, discussing the weather with the gravity reserved for matters of survival.

The chapel steps were swept. Then swept again, bristles tracing the same lines, as if repetition could erase what had settled there.

Fresh flowers appeared beneath the memorial plaque—white, small, arranged with the caution of an apology.

Inside, the chapel's air had shifted. Not lighter, but less densely packed, as if something had been released.

Vaugh stood beside me, staring at the plaque.

"They'll talk now," he said.

"Yes," I replied. "In fragments. In kitchens. In late-night whispers. Not in public."

"And that's enough?" he asked.

"It has to be," I said. "Truth is a shock here. People will take it in like medicine: in doses they can tolerate."

He looked at me.

"You alright?" he asked.

"Yes," I said. "But my brain is loud. "

He gave me the faintest smile. "Mine too."

Rhian stood at the chapel gate. She had not cried since yesterday. Her grief had thickened, settling into something weighty and functional, the way wet wool clings to the skin.

"She really thought she was protecting me," Rhian said.

"Yes," I replied.

"And she ruined everything."

"She tried to keep things from changing," I said. "But nothing stays the same. Not really."

Rhian stared down the lane, as if expecting to see the police car return and undo itself.

"My father will break," she whispered.

"He might," I said. "Sometimes breaking is not an ending. Sometimes it is only a change in form."

Rhian nodded once, very small.

"Will people hate her?" she asked.

"Some will," I said. "Because hatred is easier than accepting complicity."

"And others?"

"Others will remember the cups of tea she made after funerals," I said. "The rotas she filled, the keys she kept. They will mourn the version of her that signified order."

Rhian's mouth trembled.

"That's the part I can't understand," she whispered. "How someone can be good and still do that."

"They usually are," I said. "Very few people kill because they want to be evil. Most kill because they want to be right."

I felt Vaugh's gaze on me – a quiet, protective awareness. He didn't speak. He didn't have to.

Epilogue – The Last Note

'Some endings announce themselves. Others arrive folded and unremarked, waiting for someone to notice'.

I returned to the Black Lion to collect my bag. It was packed already; I pack early because it calms my mind to know there is at least one thing I can control.

Mrs Griffiths handed me a paper-wrapped bundle.

"Sandwich," she said. "You didn't eat enough again."

"I ate," I said.

She lifted an eyebrow in a way that suggested she did not believe definitions should be stretched that far.

Then she slid an envelope across the counter.

"This came for you," she said. "No stamp. No handwriting on the front. Just... left."

I didn't open it there.

I thanked her, touched the envelope to confirm it contained paper, not something else, then carefully put it into my bag in the compartment reserved for documents. Not because the compartment was necessary, but because routine steadies the nervous system.

Outside, the air was colder. The light had a washed-out quality. The sort that makes every surface feel too visible.

At the station, the platform smelled of damp concrete and metal. The announcement crackled incomprehensibly over the speakers. I moved to the far end of the platform. Away from the small group waiting near the benches.

I prefer edges. Edges are predictable.

When the train arrived, it was louder than expected – a sudden grinding, a hiss, a pressure change that made my ears prickle. I put on my noise-cancelling headphones, not for comfort exactly, but for function. Without them, my thoughts lose clarity when it comes to sound.

I boarded quickly, scanning for a seat with:

- A window

- No immediate neighbour

- Minimal foot traffic

The carriage was half-occupied. A child bounced on a seat behind a woman whose exhaustion was visible in the set of her shoulders. Two men debated rugby in low voices. The air carried a citrus scent, layered over something stale.

I selected a window seat, positioned my bag against my leg, and stilled myself.

The train jolted forward. The wheels established their pattern—repetitive, reliable. My shoulders released a fraction of their tension.

The man opposite leaned forward. His expression was eager, as if he considered conversation a form of benevolence.

"Off home, are you?" he asked.

I looked at him.

His smile was benign. His eyes were curious.

"Yes," I said.

He waited, as though expecting a reciprocal question.

I did not provide one.

After a moment, he filled the silence himself.

"Been away long?"

"Long enough," I said.

He laughed. "Work or pleasure?"

"Neither" I said.

His smile faltered slightly.

I considered softening my response. Experience suggests that misplaced softness generates confusion, not comfort.

He shifted, then tried again, as though this were a puzzle he could solve with enough attempts.

"Family in Wales?"

"No," I said.

"Ah," he said, still striving. "Bit of a holiday then?"

I turned to the window. Fog pressed against the fields, persistent as a memory that refuses to dissipate.

"No," I said again.

He gave up, finally, and opened his newspaper with the exaggerated relief of a man retreating into print after social failure.

I exhaled, slowly.

My body held tension during small talk in the way other bodies hold tension during danger. It is not that the questions are harmful. It is that the rules are unclear; unclear rules lead to errors, and errors have consequences.

I took the envelope from my bag.

My fingertips hovered on the flap.

I waited until the train passed through a tunnel. The sudden darkness and return to light always reset my sense of time. Then I opened it.

Inside was one sheet of paper.

Different handwriting from everything else.

Not the careful, practical hand of chapel rotas. Not the jagged fear of anonymous emails. Not the aphoristic flourish of Catrin's killer-note.

This was...controlled.

Precise.

Two lines, printed in neat capitals:

YOU SOLVED BRYNGWIN.

YOU MISSED THE PART THAT MATTERS.

I stared.

My pulse changed – not faster, exactly. Sharper. As though my nervous system had shifted from recovery into alert.

At the bottom of the page was a small symbol.

Not a signature.

A mark.

A simple shape drawn with deliberate pressure:

A triangle, intersected by a thin vertical line.

My brain tried to categorise it.

A brand?

A logo?

A child's doodle?

No – too intentional.

The man opposite cleared his throat loudly, as if reminding me he was still there. I flinched despite myself. My headphones muted the sound, but not entirely.

I folded the note and unfolded it again, aligning the edges, then misaligning them, then aligning them again. It was a regulatory action — something my hands did when my mind needed help containing itself.

YOU MISSED THE PART THAT MATTERS.

It implied:

- That I had seen a pattern, but not the whole

- That someone had been watching the investigation.

- That Bryngwyn was not an isolated case

- That the writer had knowledge beyond this village.

- And that they expected me to continue.

I stared out the window.

Fields dissolved into hedges, hedges into stone walls, stone walls into a line of trees. The train's sounds repeated, predictable. Predictability was the available comfort.

I took out my notebook and wrote three headings:

WHO

WHY

WHAT NEXT

Under **WHO**, I wrote:

- Not Carys

- Not Mrs Pritchard

- Not Vaugh

- Not the Reverend

- Someone who likes symbols

Under **WHY**, I wrote:

- Recruitment?

- Threat?

- Correction?

- Challenge?

Under **WHAT NEXT**, I wrote:

- Keep note

- Compare the symbol to any records?

- Ask Carys? (unlikely)

- Ask Carys's old archives?

Then I stopped.

Because the truth was more straightforward.

The note had done what it was designed to do.

It had intrigued me.

It had created a new pattern.

And my brain – the part that notices, the part that aligns fragments, the part that cannot leave a puzzle unfinished – had already begun to arrange itself around the next question.

The man opposite folded his newspaper and looked up again.

He smiles, attempting to re-enter.

"Interesting case was it?" he asked, nodding at my notebook.

I looked at him.

My mind generated several possible responses, most of them unsuitable for social use.

I chose the least harmful truth.

"Yes," I said. "And it appears it isn't over."

His smile faltered. "Oh."

I turned back to the window.

Outside, the world continued to move.

Inside my bag, in the compartment where paper is meant to be safe and stories are meant to conclude, the note remained. It indicated, with clarity, that some stories do neither.

They simply wait to be noticed.

Acknowledgements

This book exists because of conversations, spoken and unspoken, about truth, silence, and the stories communities tell themselves to endure.

My thanks go first to the readers who value quiet mysteries, moral complexity, and the long arc of consequences over spectacle. This book was written with you in mind.

I am grateful to those who shared their time, experiences, and patience while I asked questions about systems, memory, and how people live alongside things they would rather not name. Any errors remain my own.

Thank you to friends and family who understood that research sometimes looks like an obsession, and that long silences usually mean that the work is going well.

And finally, thank you to the places, real and imagined, that remind us how easily order can be mistaken for justice, and how often truth waits for someone willing to notice it.

About the Author

G.A. Bellingham writes mystery fiction that explores silence, systems, and the hidden patterns that shape human behaviours. Their work is characterised by psychologically precise protagonists, morally complex communities, and an interest in how truth is negotiated rather than revealed.

Anatomy of Connection is the first novel in **The Serene Mysteries** series, featuring forensic linguistic investigator Serene Pryce. Future volumes will follow Serene as individual cases begin to reveal a larger design. One that tests the limits of observation, responsibility, and how much truth a person is willing to carry.

www.ingramcontent.com/pod-product-compliance
Lightning Source LLC
Chambersburg PA
CBHW051303210726
48287CB00002B/642